DON'T FEAR THE REAPER

By
William F. Houle &
J.E. Taylor

J.E. TAYLOR
SUPERNATURAL SUSPENSE
& DARK FANTASY AUTHOR

DON'T FEAR THE REAPER

The day Nick Ramsay's eighth-grade teacher drops dead in his classroom, Nick sees his first reaper. When another cloaked figure appears at his grandmother's bedside, Nick issues an order for the vile creature to leave her alone.

This simple act of defiance creates a domino effect that brings Fate and Death to Nick's door and reveals his true lineage, throwing his world into chaos.

To make matters worse, a group of rogue reapers declares war on humanity and Nick is the only one who can stop them.

CHAPTER 1

THE FIRST TIME I saw a reaper, I thought I had fallen asleep in class again.

Mr. Sanchez was in the middle of reaming out Clyde for not having his homework for the hundredth time this year, and mid-yell, his red face turned purple and he clutched his chest.

When Mr. Sanchez fell to his knees, the sight of the black-cloaked figure behind him nearly gave *me* a heart attack. My chest burned with the sudden rush of adrenaline and my throat tingled around the scream that begged to erupt, but I clamped my lips closed.

His silver gaze peered out of the hooded darkness, staring directly at me, like he knew I could see him. His bony hand reached out and came to rest on Mr. Sanchez's head. The rotund teacher's gray eyes rolled back and his breath wheezed from his half-open mouth.

"Call nine-one-one!" The cry broke my paralysis, and I bolted to the front of the room, trying to recall the CPR instructions I had in health class last year. Thirty chest compressions then blow in the victim's mouth. The silent instructions replayed in my head, and I went into action.

It wasn't until the E.M.T.s wheeled the dead body of Mr. Sanchez out of the room that Julia took my hand for support.

"Nick, you tried," Julia said.

I looked into her golden-brown eyes and that's when I knew it wasn't a dream. Her warm hand, her soft, teary voice, cracked through my defenses and I shook. "I couldn't stop him from taking Mr. Sanchez."

"Stop who?"

I opened my mouth to speak, but before the words could tumble out, I snapped my lips closed. She was already looking at me like I had a few screws loose and this would only topple that look into the realm of disbelief. I didn't want her to think I was any crazier than she already did. I turned away, wiping my misting eyes on my sleeve.

"Stop who?" she repeated, taking my arm and swinging me toward her.

"Death, who do you think?" I snapped, my tone harsher than I wanted, harsher than I meant to be, and she recoiled. "I couldn't stop Death," I said, softening my tone and taking a deep breath to cool my nerves. "I couldn't stop Mr. Sanchez from dying."

Before she could speak, the PA system whined into action. "Dylan Nicholas Ramsay, please come to the office."

Aw, crap. What does Principal Murdock want now? I hung my head, grinding my teeth together for a moment as anger wiped away any trace of despair. "I gotta go," I said to Julia, and stepped out of her grip, trudging toward the office, wondering just what Principal Murdock was going to lay on me this time. Was he going to throw that sappy sad expression at me again, the one that always made me feel like a lost reject? The look that made me feel like crap.

Mr. Murdock offered a tight smile when I entered the office. "Nick, how are you holding up?"

Jeesh, how the Hell do you think I'm holding up? I just saw my teacher die. "I'm fine, sir."

"I think you should talk with Mrs. Lambert for a spell," Mr. Murdock said, and delivered the look I expected.

"I said I'm okay."

Mr. Murdock raised one of his wooly-mammoth eyebrows. "I understand you were yelling the entire time you were trying to revive Mr. Sanchez."

Shock slammed into my chest, drying my mouth and shooting tingling waves over my skin. "Wh-what?"

"A few of the other students said you were yelling at someone or something while you were doing CPR."

"I, uh, I don't know what you're talking about." *I knew I was cussing the Hell out of the reaper, but I didn't realize I was swearing out loud.*

"I think you should talk with Mrs. Lambert for a while."

CHAPTER 2

THE CONVERSATON WITH Mrs. Lambert went pretty much the same way, the syrupy concern and the doting questions, all of which drove me mad. I couldn't wait to get out of school and go home where it was quiet and I could lose myself in video games.

"Now Nick, you can't keep everything in," Mrs. Lambert said. Her ancient bouffant hair bobbed with the shake of her head like one of those funky bobble-head dolls you see on some people's dashboards.

I had to bite my lip to keep the laugh from rolling out and she mistook the gesture as a sign of despair, and she reached across the space, laying her wrinkled hand on top of mine.

"There, there," she said, and before she could say another word, the school bell rang and I didn't wait for her to dismiss me. Instead, I scooped up my book bag and hightailed it to the bus without a second look back.

I never thought the vinyl-clad bench would feel so good, so free, as it did today, and I closed my eyes, letting my body melt into the seat for the half-hour ride home.

"Nick?" Julia's voice interrupted the stupor I had fallen into.

I opened my eyes to her soft brown eyes so full of worry that I had to smile.

"Scoot over so I can sit down," she said, shooing me aside. When she settled in the seat, she turned toward me. "Are you really okay?"

"Yes, I'm fine. I just needed to get away from the school." I leaned over and kissed her warm cheek, catching the sweet scent of strawberry shampoo. My stomach dropped through the floor from the rush I always get when my lips touch her skin.

Her cheeks flushed, and I leaned back, studying the red hue and her almost shy smile. She settled back in the seat and took my hand for the remainder of the ride.

I closed my eyes, remembering the first time I saw her. The moving truck pulled away from the house next door and there she was, this little princess dribbling a soccer ball across the yard with her long golden hair flowing in the breeze behind her. And all I could think was, *smoking hot.*

I snuck a peek at her. She's still smoking hot after five years and she's all mine.

CHAPTER 3

I WALKED INTO the house and headed for the stairs, but a stern voice from the living room stopped my escape.

"Dylan Nicholas Ramsay, where do you think you're going?"

I turned toward my mother's voice. She stood in her nurse's uniform, with her hands on her hips and that piercing stare that makes me want to either run or spill my darkest secrets.

"What are you doing home?"

"I was able to get someone to finish my shift when I got the call from the school. Mr. Murdock said your teacher had a heart attack in class and you tried to revive him," Mom said, her tone filled with worry accompanied by those small concern lines between her eyes. "He said you were yelling at something the entire time you did CPR."

"I was yelling because I didn't want Mr. Sanchez to die and I thought if I yelled, maybe he'd hang on."

"Are you sure that's the reason?"

I rolled my eyes and sighed. "Yeah, Mom, I'm sure. Do you mind if I go play Zombie Disaster Three, now?"

"Isn't that rated for mature audiences?"

"Yeah, but all my other friends play online, too."

"Do their parents know it's rated M?"

"C'mon Mom, it's not that bad." Okay maybe it is, but I'm not telling her that, besides, I'm in the mood for a little blood and brains to block out the image of Mr. Sanchez's blue face and the hovering reaper that ripped the life from him.

"Nick, I don't want you playing that game and if I find out you are; I'll suspend your online privileges for a week."

So not the answer I was hoping for, but I knew she'd find out if I snuck onto the gaming board. I don't know how she does it, but anytime I defy her, she finds out and bam, I'm grounded. I guess I'll just have to settle for a little Medal of Honor instead. "Fine," I said, and marched up the stairs.

"Nick?"

I turned, meeting my mother's gaze.

"I'm proud of you for trying to save your teacher," she said, and sent a smile my way.

I couldn't help but smile back and I mumbled, "Thanks," before continuing to my room and swinging the door closed. I tossed my backpack in the corner before settling into my gaming chair.

Right when I was about to take down the general of the European force, my mother barged into the room and in the second I looked away, I was annihilated, shot dead by multiple enemy guns. "Mom!"

"Nick, we have to go."

The tremor in her voice tore my attention away from the game for more than a quick glimpse in her direction. What I saw in her face made me switch off the game and jump to my feet. "What's wrong?"

"Your grandmother is in the hospital."

The initial shock of those words ran through me like a stun gun and I stuttered a simple, "W-why?"

"I don't know, but they said to hurry."

The fifteen minute car ride seemed like an hour and I slumped in the seat, frightened by all the 'what if' scenarios that kept circling in my mind. At the hospital, I followed my mother through the emergency room maze to where they put my grandmother. The beeps and whooshes filled the room, echoing off the hard tile floors and gray, drab walls. Beyond the tubes and gauze and institutional blankets covering the frail form of my grandmother stood another black-cloaked figure.

Without thinking, I pointed my finger and growled a command. "You cannot have my grandmother. Leave. Now."

The hooded figure raised his silver eyes in my direction, and they transitioned into a glowing red. Although all I could see was a skeleton, I could have sworn the thing scowled at me and then it was gone.

I blinked, wondering if my shot nerves imagined the monster, and I glanced at my mother. Her gaze was glued on me, her jaw askew and her eyebrows arched with a million unasked questions.

"What?" I asked, shrugging.

"How long?" she shot back at me.

"How long what?"

"How long have you seen them?"

Stunned, I glanced back at the empty spot. "You saw that?"

Her silence pulled my attention back to her. She shook her head and swallowed, refocusing on her mother in the bed. "Is it still here?"

“No.”

My answer seemed to drain what little color remained in her cheeks and she fell into the chair, her mouth working at words that never made it past her lips. Before either of us could speak, my grandmother opened her eyes.

CHAPTER 4

THE THREE OF us walked into my grandmother's house and, after my mom tucked Gram into bed, she cornered me in the living room. "Nick, you need to tell me exactly what you saw today," she said in a hushed tone that belied her intense stare and trembling hands.

"I didn't see anything."

My mother's hands suddenly clasped my arms, her grip almost painful and her face rigid in her intent. "Nick, don't lie to me."

I should have known. Her ability to detect a lie was epic.

She released me and took a step back, taking a deep breath before framing the question again.

I didn't give her a chance. "Death, I saw Death."

Her expression became guarded in a way I have never seen. "What did he look like?"

The question threw me, and I stumbled on words, trying to describe the manifestation. "He looked like those cheesy Halloween costumes. You know. The skeleton in a black robe thing."

Concern spread into the lines in her face. "That's not what Death looks like, honey."

I raised an eyebrow. "I'm pretty sure it was Death, Mom."

"Death never wears black. What you saw was a reaper."

I rarely question my mom when she tells me something, but I saw the thing with my own eyes. I should know. "How do *you* know it wasn't Death?"

"I know."

I rolled my eyes. "Okay, Mom, whatever you say. Can we go home now?"

"Don't you roll your eyes at me, young man."

I didn't know where my mother was going with this and I didn't understand her reaction at all, but I didn't want to argue with her either. At least not at Gram's house. "I'm sorry, Mom. Can we go now?"

She glanced at the ceiling and nodded. "Just as soon as I can get a visiting nurse lined up. I'll be back down once I get that arranged and have your grandmother settled in for the night.”

I breathed a sigh of relief when my mother disappeared from view, but it was short-lived. She came back a few minutes later with that determined look that meant she would not let up on this, but at least I had a reprieve from the battery of questions until the visiting nurse arrived.

Once we were in the car, I slumped in the passenger seat and fidgeted with the zipper on my sweatshirt all the way home.

As soon as we walked into the house, my mom started in again.

“I’m sorry for getting upset with you at Grandma’s house, but I’ve seen a reaper before and they aren’t very nice, but Death is a whole other matter.”

“How do you know the difference?”

“Death is a man, not a skeleton, and he rules over the reapers,” she said.

A chill bit the air and my skin broke out in goosebumps. I wanted to ask more, but I couldn't find the words. Something about her tone told me she knew more than she was telling me and I wasn't sure I wanted to know.

"I don't really want to talk about this now, Mom." I yawned, hoping it was convincing enough to let me escape to my room. "It's been a really long day."

She sighed and nodded and I turned, trotting upstairs with both relief and dread pumping through my skin. I knew this was just the beginning and tomorrow might bring on another set of dark figures.

CHAPTER 5

PRINCIPAL MURDOCK AND Mrs. Lambert thought the entire school needed a psychology session, and they pirated our entire morning to discuss the Death of Mr. Sanchez. As the student body filtered into the auditorium, I slipped away from the crowd and snuck into the computer lab. The whir of the computer filled the room, and I kept checking the hallway for Sam, the school's security guard, sure I was going to get busted at any moment.

Google turned out to be a dead end. Yahoo wasn't any better and Ask.com just sucked balls. All I found on the internet were references to movies, gaming, myths and hearsay, nothing concrete and certainly nothing that had to do with people actually seeing reapers.

The shuffling of kids in the hallway drew my attention away from the computer and I flipped the switch, shutting the computer down before high-tailing it out of the room as fast as I could. All I needed was my mother to find out I skipped the assembly to research reapers.

Julia caught up with me in the hallway. "The principal is looking for you," she whispered in my ear and threaded her arm around mine, steering me away from the auditorium exodus.

"Why?"

"He wanted you to stand up in the auditorium. I think he was going to thank you or something, but when you didn't stand, his face turned red and he kind of laughed it off, but I could tell he was pissed."

The rest of the day, I avoided the office and any time I saw Principal Murdock; I turned the opposite direction. I thought the bus looked good yesterday, but today it signaled freedom and the start of the weekend. I smiled at Julia when she slid into the seat with me.

"Thanks for the warning this morning."

"Anytime." She flashed her sweet smile in my direction. "What are you doing this weekend?"

"I need to go to the library to finish my book report." I looked away from her. She didn't know I had already finished the assignment last weekend.

"Do you mind if I come with you?"

I turned back to her, unsure of how to answer, but her brown eyes melted my resolve and I swallowed the lie, smiling and nodding. As much as I needed to research the mysterious dark figures I kept seeing, I also needed to spend some time with her. "Sure, I'll call you when I'm ready to go."

Her arm laced through mine and she leaned her head on my shoulder for the rest of the ride, content to let the silence settle between us. I kissed the top of her head, thankful for her attention and tolerance, and closed my eyes, lulled to sleep by the hum of the engine and the comfort of her sweet scent.

CHAPTER 6

I STOOD ON a plateau, darkness surrounding me like a warm blanket until a sea of hooded figures turned toward me. Their burning gaze sent fiery chills up my spine and through my extremities until I shivered. I turned to flee, and instead I teetered on the edge of a gorge, the drop endless and black beyond rocks that jutted out, jagged like *a set of claws made for tearing the flesh off young boys stupid enough to jump.*

Either way I turned, certain death awaited.

Fear stroked my shaking form, creating a panic as feral as a cornered bear and I spun back to the crowd of reapers...

...and sat straight up in the seat with Julia shaking my arm. "Nick, wake up, we're home. This is our stop."

I blinked and wiped my eyes, grabbed my backpack and followed her off the bus, still in a stupor, with my heart banging a new hip-hop tune in my chest. The dream was still as vivid as the bite in the air. I tried to shake it, but the disturbing vision clung like a leach.

"Are you okay?" Julia asked.

"Yeah. I'm just having a hard time waking up." I started the short trek home with her hand clasped in mine. The brisk spring wind wound through the streets, shuffling the lush trees and blowing the blooming flowers, demanding they bend to its force.

"You want to come over for a while?"

"Sure, but I need to stop at home and drop my backpack off." Julia's mother always had fresh cookies or pies on hand, and I wasn't thrilled about going into an empty house, especially after the nightmare. Besides, the pit stop offered a chance to be alone with Julia. Maybe I'd even get to second base this time.

The thought made me smile, and I stole a glance at Julia. She sent her secret smile back in my direction, telling me we were both on the same page. I couldn't help the thunderous patter of my heart and as we rounded the last corner, all I could think of was the feel of her lips.

My mother's car sat in the driveway, along with a silver sports car I didn't recognize, and I stopped walking. "I thought my mom was working." I traded a glance with Julia. The same disappointment pounding in my veins reflected in her eyes.

Fear rocketed to the forefront of my mind, and my mouth ran dry. I broke out in a run, darting across the street with a cursory glance. Julia's feet slapped the pavement in her bid to keep up, but I didn't slow and flew into the house, sliding to a stop in the entry. Julia slammed into me and I teetered out of balance for a second before catching myself and putting my finger to my lips.

My mother's voice carried through the house and I knew the terse tone. She wasn't happy with whoever owned the car outside. I tiptoed toward the kitchen, with Julia's hand clasped in mine.

"Why, Dylan? Why now? I thought you said he wouldn't be affected until he was eighteen?"

"I don't know," a deep voice penetrated the walls. "He shouldn't be seeing them. Not yet."

I peeked around the corner, trying to catch a glimpse of the man behind the musical timbre. He looked like he'd just stepped off an island cruise, with light kakis and a pastel yellow shirt that made his modest tan stand out. His dark hair reached his shoulders, curling every which way, like my hair right after it dried. When his weathered face turned in my direction, my breath caught at the blue-green glow of his eyes, hypnotizing and calming at the same time.

Julia shivered as his gaze passed over her and she pulled her hand from mine, backing out of the house like she had seen a ghost. Caught between intrigue and worry, I hesitated, wondering if I should go after Julia or step into full view of my mother.

"But..." my mother started, and the man raised his hand, stopping her and nodding in my direction. She spun, gawking at me with wide eyes. "What are you doing sneaking around like that?"

I stepped into view and shrugged. "I, um, I didn't recognize the car…" I said, still trying to make heads or tails of their conversation. My gaze traveled to the stranger in my kitchen and back to her.

"How long have you been there?"

"Not very long."

She sighed and traded a glance with the man. "Nick, this is Mr. Mckay, and he was just leaving."

Mr. Mckay raised a questioning eyebrow. "Holly, this conversation is far from over."

"Dylan, please just go."

For a moment, I thought she was talking to me, but her gaze didn't leave his and I had never seen her eyes pleading like that with anyone before. *Who is this guy?* Mr. Mckay broke the stare and swung his gaze to mine like he heard the question.

"I'll let your mother explain that. Right now, I need to swing in and see your grandmother."

My mom's face blanched, and she grabbed Mr. Mckay's arm. "Dylan." Her voice shook. He glanced back at her.

"Holly, it's her time and I need to do damage control before they get out of hand."

"But it's my mother."

"I know. That's why I'm going," he put his hand over hers and sighed. "There's dissention in the ranks and if I don't correct this, it will be all out war."

"Correct what?" I was now more confused than ever.

"Please," my mother pleaded.

"If I don't, they'll come after my son," he said softly, but I still caught it, followed by the immediate reaction of my mother. Her gaze sought mine and then jumped back to the man in front of her and she shook her head, letting go of Mr. Mckay.

The realization struck me like a two-ton truck slamming into a brick wall, and I reached for the counter. I stared at the man and then at my mother. "Who is he?"

"Nicky," my mother started, and I grit my teeth.

She only called me Nicky when she wanted to avoid the subject. Anger brewed under my skin and I stood straight and pointed at Mr. Mckay. "Who the Hell is he?"

Mr. Mckay's eyes sparked, and he stepped toward me, towering. "You will not talk to your mother that way."

Fear shot through me like a razor slicing through my soul, but I stood my ground. "Who are you to tell me what I can and can't do?" I shot the question, not really wanting to know the answer, but challenging the anger I saw in his narrowing eyes.

"Don't," my mother yelled, but she wasn't quick enough.

His words spilled from his lips over her protest. "I'm your father." He grabbed my arm.

Tingles spread from his touch through every fiber of my body and I stared at his unearthly eyes, drowning in their depths just before the world went black.

CHAPTER 7

HUSHED VOICES PULLED me from the dark void. Foggy beings hovered over me and I blinked until my vision righted. My mother sent a strained smile in my direction before looking over at the man standing next to her.

"I told you he'd be okay," Mr. Mckay said.

I studied the man who said he was my father and when his gaze turned to mine, I shivered. Something about him struck me as ominous and dangerous, but right under that façade, I saw something deeper, less scary. Pulling myself into a sitting position, I broke eye contact and looked at the floor trying to figure out what just happened.

"So, you're my father."

"Yes." He took a seat next to me and glanced at my mother before focusing back on me. "And my last name isn't McKay. It's Ramsay."

I opened my mouth but with so many questions flying through my mind, I couldn't pick just one, so instead I sighed and turned my gaze to him.

"I left because I had no choice, Nick. It wasn't because I didn't want to be with you and your mom."

His answer pissed me off because you *always* have a choice. "What do you mean you had no choice?"

"It comes with the job."

"What the Hell kind of job do you have?"

"Dylan Nicholas Ramsay!" my mother scolded.

My father raised his hand, stopping my mother. "He has a right to be upset, Holly. He doesn't know me from Adam, and I had the same reaction when my father showed up. Fortunately for Nick, he's got a hell of a lot more time to learn the ropes than I did."

The icy tendrils of fear scratched my skin, and I broke out in a rash of goosebumps accompanied by another shiver. I thought I wanted an explanation, but now I wasn't so sure and when his gaze swung to mine, I knew I'd rather be left in the dark.

"I'm sorry, son, but the truth of the matter is, you're destined to follow in my footsteps. There is no choice." He shrugged and glanced at my mother.

"And what exactly does that mean?" I scooted to the corner of the couch, as far away from the man next to me as I could get.

"It means when you turn twenty-five, you take over my job."

"What exactly is your job?"

My mother stepped closer and touched his shoulder, a silent plea in her eyes stopping my father from expanding further. He covered her hand and brought it to his lips, and I saw the compassion and love he felt for her in this simple move. "He needs to know."

"Know what?"

"Who I am," he said.

I waited, raising a questioning eyebrow because as much as my mind was screaming to run, to hide, to deny the truth, I couldn't help the curiosity that took control.

"Simply put, I'm Death with a capital D."

I was not prepared for his answer and I blinked, trying to reconcile the information I dug up on reapers and Death and the history of these beings, and this man. This manifestation was nowhere near what I expected. Then the follow up realization hit like a bomb.

My father is Death.

Holy shit.

Still trying to wrap my head around his words, I stuttered, "Y-y-you don't look like a reaper."

"I'm not a reaper. Reapers collect the souls on the master list when I need them to."

The nightmare on the bus surfaced in my mind and I looked away from my father. Those reapers weren't there to do my bidding, they were there to destroy me. I glanced back at him and his eyes widened.

"A nightmare?"

His statement sent a wave of unease over me, and my stomach tightened into a knot of pain. I clenched my teeth against the thin stream of bile burning my throat, swallowing and nodding at the same time. He was in my head, hearing my thoughts, seeing my nightmares, and that didn't settle well.

Dimples appeared briefly and his eyes flashed. "That comes with the job, too." His smile faded. "I have to go fix something, but I'll be back and we can talk then. Okay?"

Thoughts swirled, and I glanced at my mother. The sad expression traced on her face brought focus to the reality of his words and my gaze snapped back to him. "Not Gram."

"Yes. I'm afraid it's her time and when you ordered that reaper away, it set some nasty things in motion on this side of the realm. I have to fix it, otherwise a few in the ranks will go rogue and that's dangerous, son."

"If it's dangerous for me, I'm okay with that if it means my grandmother lives," I said, remembering the conversation I overheard in the kitchen and unwilling to swap my grandmother's life for my safety.

"I'm afraid it's not just that simple, Nick."

"Why not?"

"Because if the reapers go rogue, there will be more death and destruction than you can imagine." He stood and turned to my mother. "Stay here." He walked out the door before I could collect my thoughts and stop him.

I ran after him, but by the time I got to the driveway, his taillights disappeared around the corner.

CHAPTER 8

I SAT WITH my mother, holding her hands while she cried, both of us mourning the Death of Gram in our own ways. The call hadn't come, and my father hadn't returned, but we both knew Gram's soul was being escorted to a better place. After what seemed like hours, my mother wiped her face and glanced at the clock. Her eyebrows knit together and she crossed to the phone, dialing without looking in my direction.

"Mom?" Surprise laced her voice and when she turned toward me, her face reminded me of the gray ash in the fireplace. A chill settled over the room and the concern in my mother's eyes sent my heart into a staccato drumbeat.

She turned away and settled into a chair, her posture tense as she did her best to engage in small talk. After a few minutes she cut the call short, blaming it on me, and after she hung up, she crossed and took a seat across from me, her hands kneading together like a mini-wrestling match.

"Gram's okay?"

She nodded and inhaled, her chest inflating and deflating slowly before she spoke. "Yes, and I'm not sure why."

"Maybe my father changed his mind."

Mom looked beyond me out the front window and sighed. "Maybe."

Her tone didn't convince either of us and when her gaze finally landed back on me, I knew she didn't believe it. That worry crease was back between her eyes, and she offered a tight smile. "You should head over to Julia's for a while."

"Are you going to Gram's?"

She hesitated and looked toward the door, the conflict visible in the tension in her neck and jaw, and then she nodded. "But I'm not sure it's safe for you to go."

"Why wouldn't it be?"

"Because if something's happened to your father..."

I waited for her to finish, but she just drifted off, pressing her lips against any scenario those words led to. Finally, I prodded her to complete her thought. "Really, Mom? He's Death, what could happen?" I refrained from rolling my eyes at her.

Her brows arched and her head cocked to the side for a moment before she laughed and the lines creasing her forehead smoothed. "I guess you could come with me."

My stomach clenched, and fear stroked my skin, creating a chill that was colder than an iceberg. I forced a smile, wondering what was wrong with me. I loved my grandmother's house. It always reminded me of chocolate chip cookies and apple pie, so why in the world was I afraid?

CHAPTER 9

WHEN WE ENTERED Gram's house, the warmth wrapped around us like a summer day and we glanced at each other before heading toward the delectable scent of chocolate. Gram stood next to the stove, stirring a pan of fudge, and she glanced over her shoulder with a smile. "They said you would be coming over, so I thought a fresh batch of fudge would be just what the doctor ordered."

"Who told you we were coming?" Mom asked, her tone guarded.

"The nice men who came by earlier. I'm sure you saw them on your way in. They left right when you arrived. Stood right there and said you'd be coming over and I should bake something nice for you." Gram waved the chocolate-covered spoon toward the dining room, splattering the refrigerator and floor with dark drops. The action was so unlike my grandmother that I shivered and my gaze snapped to where she pointed.

Two figures stood in the shadows, their red eyes burning into me, and the scowls on their skeletal faces relayed their dark intent. I wanted to run, but my feet wouldn't listen to reason. They stayed planted in the same spot, like they were wrapped in lead. My voice caught in my throat and I couldn't pull my gaze away from their sinister expressions.

"I didn't see anyone, Mom. Why don't you let me finish making the fudge and you go lay down in the living room, okay?" To my mother's credit, her voice didn't shake nor did she show any signs of fear, but somehow I knew her heart was knocking in her chest as hard as mine was. Terror radiated from her, but for different reasons than the potent panic filling my bones.

The reapers weren't here for us. No, they were here to stand as a warning. A warning of just how easily they could slip into our lives and yank anyone we cared about at a whim. Their warning was simple. "Do not interfere in the war we are about to wage."

I had no idea if my father was okay or not, but they had set this trap and we walked right into it. That turned my fear into liquid fury burning through my veins. "Where's my father?" The question came out in a low growl despite the deep-seated dread pummeling my chest.

The reaper closest to me pointed his bony finger at me, and a voice that I could only categorize as a squeak from hell filled the house. "That is not your concern."

"Let him go." It wasn't a question or a plea. I gave an order, and I was certain they had to follow it.

Laughter rang in my ears. "You have no power over us, boy."

"Tell me what you did with my father." My hands balled into tight fists against my thighs and I willed them to speak, to spill the secret.

"He's in Purgatory, guarded by Leviathan."

"Who's Leviathan?"

"He guards the Gates of Hell."

"Are you telling me my father's in Hell?"

The reaper chuckled and disappeared.

I stood, stunned, staring at the empty space in the dining room doorway. Shuffling noises behind me caught my attention, and I spun to find my mother's wide-eyed gaze locked on me, and her knuckles white from her death grip on the doorframe. "What did they say?" Her voice quivered, and I knew she heard my side of the conversation, but her mind just wasn't equipped to piece it together, not after the last few hours of chaos.

"They took him to Purgatory." I didn't think her face could turn the shade of gray-green that reminded me of the walls in the boy's bathroom at school and I moved on instinct, reaching for her as she collapsed. I caught her and put her on the ground as gracefully as possible and I was able to lay her down without slamming her head against the wall or the floor.

Her eyes fluttered open, and she glanced around the room like she didn't know where she was and when her gaze landed on me, she bit her lip and her eyes filled with tears. "Did you say Purgatory?"

"That's what they said."

"What else did they say?"

"They're waging a war and they expect me to stay out of it, but I can't. I need to figure out how to rescue my father and stop this war."

"How?" She sat up. "How in the world can you stop them?"

"I don't know yet, but I will."

CHAPTER 10

AFTER WE GOT Gram settled, we headed back home, and I disappeared into my room and booted up my computer, determined to figure anything that would give me a clue on how to stop a reaper. I knew facts would be thin to nothing, but maybe there would be an old wives' tale or urban legend that had a grain of truth.

My stomach rumbled, and I glanced at the clock, blinking and rubbing my eyes at the flashing numbers. It was almost eight and my mom hadn't called me down for dinner like she usually does. I swung the chair around and froze halfway to my feet. I had been so deep in the research that I never heard my mother come in. She left a tray with a ham and cheese sandwich, an apple, and a bag of chips, along with my favorite soda on my bed a few feet away from my desk.

I grabbed the sandwich and sat back in the chair, swiveling toward the computer with a sigh. I hadn't found a thing online. In everything I looked at, if the article didn't have to do with music or gaming, then it rambled about religion. I took a bite of the sandwich and turned that over in my mind. Mid-chew, I stopped and almost palmed my forehead.

Religion.

A priest. I should talk to a priest.

I finished the rest of the sandwich in two bites and swiped the soda off the tray on my way out of my room. "Mom?" I yelled from the top of the stairs and descended into the well-lit family room where my mother was channel surfing.

She muted the television and glanced at me. She raised an eyebrow, inviting me to continue.

"I think I need to talk to Father Michael."

Both eyebrows arched. "Why?"

"I think he might be able to help me."

My mother's expression didn't change. It remained frozen in perpetual surprise and I thought for a moment the world stopped spinning until she blinked and pressed her lips together. The thin line of her mouth and deep scrunch between her eyes expressed her concern, but more than that, I could almost hear the whisper of her thoughts.

"Don't worry, I won't tell him who my father is."

The lines smoothed, followed by an audible sigh of relief. "You really think he can help?"

I shrugged. I wasn't certain of anything, but it was better than spinning my wheels at the computer. "It has to be better than just doing random Google searches."

"I have to work tonight, but you can give Father Michael a call if you'd like. If he isn't available, we can stop in and see him tomorrow."

"Okay, but I'm supposed to go to the library with Julia tomorrow. Think we can talk to Father Michael before I go?"

"Let me know if you get a hold of him. If not, I'll call him first thing in the morning and see if we can swing by the rectory."

"Thanks, Mom." I tried Father Michael while she got ready for work. All I got was the answering machine, and I hung up without leaving a message. I'd try again later and instead, plopped myself on the couch. The minute I got settled in the soft cushions, my eyelids drooped from the stress of the day. It didn't take long before the lull of the television sucked me into another dream.

CHAPTER 11

I FIDGETED IN the chair in the rectory office while my mother spoke with Father Michael in the hallway. Their hushed whispers echoed against the marble, and I waited for them to enter the room. My mother hung back in the hallway when Father Michael entered and she gave me that strained smile I knew too well. She wanted to make sure I kept my promise. She didn't want me to reveal who my father was, and I sent her a nod, letting her know I would keep silent. She sent a more natural smile my way and disappeared from the doorway to wait in the car.

"Your mother said you've been having some adjustment issues since your teacher died. Did you want to talk about it?" Father Michael said. He crossed to the couch next to me and took a seat, his black robes billowing from his girth before they settled neatly around his rotund belly. Father Michael reminded me of Friar Tuck in the old Robin Hood movies, except instead of a brown frock, he wore black, making his white collar stand out like a beacon.

I shrugged, keeping up the pretense that we had discussed. "I've been having nightmares about reapers lately," I said, glad it wasn't a lie. I'm not sure there would be enough Hail Mary's to absolve me of that kind of sin and I hoped God would understand the partial truths and subterfuge I was about to lay on the kind priest.

"Reapers?"

"Yes, and I was curious as to where they come from and why?"

"Reapers are agents of Death, son."

"I figured that much out, but do you know where they come from? Like where I can find them?"

Father Michael leaned back into the fabric of the couch and folded his hands over his belly as he studied me, his face scrunched in contemplation. "Why would you want to find an agent of Death?"

"I saw one when Mr. Sanchez died."

Silence filled the room, and Father Michael's eyes narrowed as he studied me. "You saw a reaper?"

"Yes, sir."

"Usually, only those near the end can see Death."

"It wasn't Death. It was a skeletal figure in a black robe. A reaper. And I was trying to revive Mr. Sanchez, so technically, I was near death." I could tell my analogy confused him.

"What was this figure doing?"

"The reaper placed his hand on Mr. Sanchez's head and then he died. I tried to save him, but I was too late."

Father Michael leaned forward. "Did you see anything else?"

"No. One minute the reaper was there and Mr. Sanchez was alive, and the next the reaper was gone and Mr. Sanchez was dead." I could feel the impatience building in my belly, clawing at the walls of my skin just dying to break free.

But I harnessed it, using the silence to focus on what had already been said.

Those near the end.

I blinked and almost laughed aloud. I now knew where to find reapers and I prayed when I found one, it wouldn't be the nasty bastards from my grandmother's house. I prayed it would listen and could help me stop the pending disaster.

"So, no bright lights or dark tunnels?"

"No. Sorry." I could tell he wanted more just by the way he sat on the edge of the couch and the light of curiosity dancing in his eyes. "What do you know about Purgatory?" I asked, changing the subject and silencing the sudden flood of questions swarming in his head.

He blinked rapidly as if I dropped the f-bomb or something and then his mouth opened and closed in indecision while his mind raced to catch up. Father Michael pressed his lips together and settled back on the couch. "Purgatory is neither Heaven nor Hell. It's a plane in between, a waiting room of sorts."

"Are you sure it isn't a part of Hell?"

"I've got no reason to believe it is. Why do you ask?"

I noodled on this for a moment before asking my next question, "Well, if Purgatory is the waiting room to Heaven or Hell, then wouldn't both the Pearly Gates and the Gates of Hell actually be in Purgatory?"

His eyebrows arched as he considered my question. "That's an interesting deduction, and I don't have a cut and dry answer for you."

"What about Leviathan?"

A crease appeared between Father Michael's eyes and I knew I had gone too far. "Nick, I believe you are deliberately changing subjects on me."

I bit my lip and dropped my gaze to my hands.

"Death is a natural part of life, son."

My gaze snapped to his. "I know."

"Then why don't you tell me what's really bothering you?"

He knew I was on a digging expedition, I could see it in his eyes and instead of dancing this fine line, I hit him head on. "What would happen if a pair of reapers went rogue? To, like, go off script."

My question left Father Michael speechless. His mouth even dropped open at the prospect and each time he opened his mouth to answer, he reconsidered and shifted in the seat. Finally, he said, "That would be very bad."

"How would you stop them?"

This question raised Father Michael's eyebrows, so they rivaled the McDonald's arches and I had to put the nix on my sudden need to chuckle. He stood and crossed to the window with his hands clasped behind his back, contemplating.

"Father Michael?"

"Nick, I'm a little worried about this line of questioning," he said, and then silence blanketed the room.

I waited until my nerve endings shouted for me to act. "Why?"

He turned and stared at me. "This is much more serious than your mother led me to believe."

His train of thought broadcasted into my head like the static filled AM news channel that my mother listened to from time to time and I stiffened at the direction he was heading. "I'm not delusional, Father Michael." It was only after I spoke I realized I was actually hearing what Father Michael was thinking. This fresh development sent tendrils of shock through my body, and I missed what Father Michael asked.

"Well?"

"Well, what?" I asked, hoping he'd repeat the question because the static in my head silenced.

"I asked if I had been asking the type questions you are, what would you think?"

I saw his point and laughed. "I would think the kid belonged in the nuthouse."

"See my predicament?"

"Yes." I leaned back into the cushion, thinking this was a mistake.

"But I have seen some strange things in my lifetime. Things that can't be explained by logic or science, so I'm not discounting that you saw what you believed to be a reaper."

His admission caught me off guard, and I stared at the portly priest, discounting my prior thoughts.

"Are the reapers after you?" he asked.

I shook my head. "No," I added.

He crossed slowly to the couch, his brow creased in thought and when his gaze landed on me, I squirmed under the conflict I saw there. He sat and leaned forward so there were only a few inches of space between us. "I've heard plenty of tales in my lifetime, half of which were complete hoaxes, but not once has anyone asked me how to stop a reaper. You realize you're asking how to stop Death, right?"

"No. If your time is up, there's nothing you can do to stop Death. What I'm asking is how to stop a reaper gone rogue."

"How would you know if a reaper has gone rogue?"

I couldn't answer that question, at least not without ending up in a padded cell. "Let's just say he did. How would someone stop him?"

Father Michael sat back and rubbed his chin. "I don't have an answer for you, Nick."

I offered a smile and a nod. "Well, thank you for talking to me today, but I promised my girlfriend we'd go to the

library and work on our book reports."
I stood, not wanting to say anymore,
and I was a little disheartened to find
that Father Michael had no answers,
no nugget of information that would
help stop the monsters.

CHAPTER 12

I STARED OUT the window as my mother drove home. She didn't ask any questions until she parked in the driveway, and then she turned in my direction and started the grand inquisition.

"Stop, Mom!" I yelled after the fiftieth question fired my way.

"What did Father Michael say?"

"He doesn't have a clue how to stop a rogue reaper. But he gave me an idea of where I can find a reaper." I opened the door to escape the confines of the car.

She grabbed my arm, and I hesitated, looking back at her worried gaze. "Nick..."

"Mom, I told you, I need to stop this war and the only way I can think of to stop them is to find an ally who knows something about reapers."

"There has to be another way," she said.

"I don't think there is another way and if I do nothing, a lot of innocent people will die." I finally said it out loud and the responsibility of the statement hit with the full force of a hurricane. I melted into the seat with the weight of it.

"Nick, this isn't your fight."

But it was, and whether or not she liked it, I had to see it through. Instead of worrying her, I just nodded and slipped out of the car. While I wanted to just stick my head in the sand and forget about the last few days, I couldn't.

I glanced toward Julia's house and she waved to me from her front porch. I sent her a wave and retrieved my backpack from the front hallway.

"Mom, I'm heading over to Julia's for a while, okay?" I announced and didn't wait for the answer. I just took off, leaving her at the front door with thoughts of danger racing around in her mind.

"Hey, Nick," Julia smiled and stood as I approached her front steps. "Are you okay?"

I nodded and dropped my bag on the stairs, pulling her to me in a warm hug. I closed my eyes and inhaled, losing myself in her sweet scent. Her body molded to mine, warming the cold center of dread in my stomach.

"Who was that at your house yesterday?"

I stiffened in her arms and pulled away, avoiding her gaze. Instead, I looked at my house and shoved my hands in my pockets, unsure of how to answer her.

"Did he have something to do with your grandmother?"

"No." I shifted my weight and looked back at her. "Not directly." I fidgeted, uncomfortable with the way she was studying me, just waiting. Instead of answering, I picked up my bag. "You ready to head to the library?"

"Nick."

I turned back to her. "What?"

"He scared me," she whispered.

The innocence of that comment made me smile. Death should scare her. He had no right to be around such a beautiful girl. "I know. You ran out of the house like it was on fire."

She smacked my arm, and the humor lit up her eyes. "Now you're just making fun of me."

"Ayup." I grinned at her and hooked my arm around her waist, leading her down the walkway.

We made it halfway to the library before she asked again. "Seriously, who was that man?"

I sighed. "That was my father."

Julia stopped. "Your what?"

"Turns out my father is alive and well and he decided to pay us a visit." I kept walking, afraid of actually seeing her reaction. It took a moment before her hand grabbed the crook of my arm, yanking me around to face her. Shock outlined her wide eyes underlined by a subtle shade of fear and I offered a smile I was sure would just stoke those fires.

"Your father is alive?"

Debatable, but I wasn't about to say that out loud, instead I nodded.

"He smells like a fire."

Reverting to all the stories I was told growing up, I shrugged. "He was a firefighter. My mom told me he died when the World Trade Center collapsed." He and his entire unit perished when the North tower fell and now I wondered how much of that was true or whether he was there to shepherd them to whatever comes next after your heart stops beating.

I realized the latter was probably more of the truth than what my mom told me, but now I was curious. I filed that question away for later tonight and focused back on Julia. She was talking, and I missed what she said.

"I'm sorry, Jules, I'm still a little out of it. This whole thing is screwing with my mind."

She offered a hint of a smile and wrapped her arm around mine. "I bet. I thought he died?"

We crossed Main Street, heading toward the library, and I glanced at the sign for York Hospital and slowed my pace. I needed to find a reaper, but I didn't want to drag Julia into it.

"What's wrong?"

I turned back toward Julia. "Nothing." Then I glanced at the sign again. "I just need to make a quick stop before we go to the library." I pointed toward the hospital and got a raised eyebrow in response.

"The hospital?"

I nodded without an explanation and prayed she wouldn't push for an answer.

"What's at the hospital?"

Looks like God was ignoring my prayers these days. "I need to see if I can find someone, but I'll drop you off at the library first."

"I don't mind going with you."

Julia liked an adventure, and the hospital qualified as just that for her. I knew there was only one way to discourage her. "It's my father…"

Her footfalls slowed, and I glanced at her, wondering just how much meeting him had affected her. I got my answer a moment later with an attempt at a smile. "I guess I could wait at the library for you."

I escorted her down the hill between the Dairy Mart and Rick's Café parking lots to the library. I savored the feel of her soft, warm lips on mine in the entryway and when I broke contact, an emptiness filled the space warmth had occupied. "I won't be long," I said, and before I could change my mind, I headed out toward the hospital.

CHAPTER 13

THE HOSPITAL STUNK like antiseptic and old people, and I didn't know which one gave me more of the willies. I walked through the emergency room, thinking I would get pulled aside at every glance, but I wasn't stopped. They didn't even give me more than a cursory look until I started toward the operating rooms.

Then nurses and other hospital personnel swarmed like gnats on a pile of fresh seaweed.

"Where do you think you're going?" A nurse wearing purple scrubs hurried from behind the check-in desk.

I sent her my best innocent, embarrassed smile, the one I usually reserve for my basketball teammates when I've made a stupid foul, and tried to remember the term for critical patients. *Intensive care—that's it.* "I'm looking for the intensive care unit. My grandmother is there, and I got lost coming back from the cafeteria," I said, hoping she wouldn't insist on looking her up on the computer like they had the other night.

"These are the operating rooms. You want to take the elevator to the third floor and follow the blue line." She pointed to the colored lines on the floor that led to the different areas of the hospital.

"Thank you." I turned and retraced my steps to the elevator, and took it to the intensive care unit. This time, I waited in the shadows until the attending nurse stepped away from the desk. I slipped past and stood in the center of the hallway, scanning the number of doors lining the walls, and inhaled. My gaze kept pulling to the third door on the right and I stepped toward it. Before I stepped inside the room, I did a quick check of both ends of the hall and then I slid inside, closing the door and blinking to adjust to the minimal light. The wheeze of the oxygen machine overrode the blood rushing in my ears and I focused on the patient in the bed.

My first reaction was I had made a mistake. This was a kid, a young kid, and sleeping in the corner was a haggard-looking woman who looked both young and old at the same time. The more my eyes adjusted, the clearer the scene before me became, and my gaze snapped to the figure blending with the shadows.

A reaper. And it was staring at me.

"I can see you," I whispered and the woman in the chair stirred, but didn't wake.

The reaper lifted a finger to its mouth, both signaling and whispering for me to be quiet.

I raised an eyebrow. This reaper's voice was soft and pleasant and full of warmth, unlike the reapers I saw earlier at my grandmother's. *I need to talk to you,* I thought, hoping the figure would hear me as if I spoke.

The being glanced between me and the girl in the bed and back, pointing in the child's direction.

I'm not here to stop you from doing your job, but it is urgent that I speak with you.

The reaper pointed toward the hall and then disappeared. I stepped outside, glancing in both directions and not seeing the reaper. I was about to open the door again when I heard a distinct hiss. I scanned the hall again and saw a girl with jet-black hair waving to me from a cracked door. I did another quick scan of my surroundings and then hustled to the room, slipping inside before the on-duty nurse looked up from whatever she was doing at the desk.

Darkness blanketed me and I fumbled for a light switch as my heart jumped in my chest. My fingers found the button and I pushed it. Bright lights blinded me and I squinted at the girl across the closet from me.

"You said you needed to talk. So talk," she said, and this time her tone carried an impatient quality.

"How," I started and swallowed, "how come you've got a body now?"

She glanced toward the wall and then back at me. "I thought it might be easier for you to talk to me in this form. I can strip the illusion if you'd prefer."

"No, no, that's fine." I didn't know how to start, so I stuck out my hand. "I'm Nick," I introduced.

She stared at the offered hand and then raised her gaze. "You know what I am, right?"

"You're a reaper."

She nodded.

I kept my hand out, willing her to shake it. I had to know if I was immune to her touch or if I would swoon into blackness like when my father touched me.

"I'm Isabel." She tepidly stretched her fragile hand out and wrapped it around mine. Her touch was cool but not unpleasant, and the initial shock of contact wore off quickly, but her eyes widened and she yanked her hand away like I had burned her.

"Who are you?"

"My name's Nick and you know my father."

A crease appeared between her eyes and she tilted her head, studying me. Unlike the other reapers, she didn't seem to be able to get in my head very far. Before she could speak, her gaze snapped to the right. "Don't go anywhere," she said, and evaporated in a swirl of steam.

Out in the hall, I could hear the fast patter of footsteps and the muted singular tone of a heart monitor, and I knew where my reaper had gone. I wanted to go to the room, to see the transition, but instead, I waited for her to return, knowing that if I saw her take the girl's spirit, I might be tempted to stop her and then the domino effect of my mistake would compound.

The soft sobs of the girl's mother drifted down the hall and I leaned my forehead against the door, closing my eyes, trying to block out the sorrow overwhelming me. I blinked and wiped at my face, shocked to see the wet proof of tears. This was not like me. I don't cry.

"Who is your father?"

Her voice sent shock waves through me and I spun, almost losing my balance. Reaching for the nearest shelf, I caught myself and stared at her red-rimmed eyes and the tears flowing freely down her pale cheeks.

"Dylan," I said, unsure of why I used his name instead of just saying Death, but the result was the same. Her jaw dropped, and she stepped backwards, putting distance between us.

"That's...that's impossible."

I wanted to laugh. So many things in the last few days were impossible, just like this bizarre conversation. "Oh, believe me, it's possible. He's missing, and I need your help."

"What do you mean, missing?"

"A couple of reapers have taken him to Purgatory and right now, I don't think we have time to go get him. Those reapers are waging war, and I need to know how to stop them."

"War?"

"Look, Isabel, can you help me or not?"

Her face hardened, and she crossed her arms. "I don't care much for your tone."

I rolled my eyes and shook my head. Of all the reapers in the universe, I had to get one with an attitude. "Look, if you can't help me, I need to find someone who can because if I don't stop them, many who aren't supposed to die will."

Her eyes widened as the situation sank in and she stepped closer. "Only your father can stop them."

"They said Leviathan is guarding him," I said, as if I really knew what that meant.

"Oh shi...shoot." Isabel turned away from me and sighed. "I can try to help, but depending on who it is, I might be just as useless as a ghost would be."

"How do I stop them?" I asked, and she grabbed my wrist. This time, the touch produced a heat that glided up my arm like an inferno.

"You take your place at the head of the table," she answered, and the burning spread into my shoulder and chest.

I spun into ippon and flipped her over my back onto the ground, cutting whatever she was doing off. Blinking, I stared down at her shocked expression. "It's not my time and you damn well know it." The transition into the dark figure was instant. The thing loomed over me and when it spoke, I knew they had intercepted Isabel.

It cackled in that deep threatening way and reached for me.

I stepped back, and the doorknob wedged into the small of my back, offering an escape route. I took it, swiveling and ripping the door open before the reaper could lay a finger on me. I ran and skidded to a stop. Blocking the elevator was the other reaper, and he was holding onto Isabel, despite her best efforts to break free.

"Let her go," the order slid from my lips formed in a low growl and the being complied, stunned for a moment at its inability to hold on to my only ally. Isabel took flight down the stairwell and I followed, sensing her as opposed to seeing her.

The moment we hit the street, she took human form again, matching me stride for stride as I headed toward the library. "You said I know your father," she said just before I reached the door.

"Yes." I glanced at her and sighed. "I'm Dylan's son."

She grabbed my arm. "By Dylan, do you mean Death?"

I nodded, and she dropped her hand.

"No wonder you didn't go into cardiac arrest when I touched you."

"I guess that's a good thing." I turned away from the door, scanning the woods surrounding the back of the library. "They have my dad and they don't want me to interfere in their war."

"There have been some rumors, but I didn't think they'd go through with it." The words came out in a rush of air and I didn't look at her.

I just stared straight ahead and offered another quick nod.

"Holy cow."

"How do I stop them?"

It was Isabel's turn to look away. "If they've imprisoned your father, there is little we can do, because unless they destroy him, you're vulnerable. I'm not sure why they haven't come after you yet, but they will. You're the last in the royal bloodline."

"Royal bloodline?"

"Yes. Death's bloodline traces back to the ancient druids and the first priest kings of humanity. It was then that the Archangels chose the Angel of Death from the human population to rule over the legion of reapers and do Fate's bidding. The future is already written and there have been very few times that Death has wavered from the path because the consequences are brutal. If you piss off Fate, she has a tendency to rip up the playbook and erase civilizations."

I slid my gaze to her again, looking for some sign that she was feeding me a line of bull. But her eyes carried a faraway look that seemed truly genuine.

"Death is Heaven's most revered angel because he was born of human blood and his power in the wrong hands could lay waste to your world."

CHAPTER 14

THE SILENCE OF the library unnerved me as much as the current situation, and to complicate things further, Death's apprentice accompanied me and she looked like the type of teenage girl I would go for if I wasn't hooked up with Julia. The farther into the library we moved, the more I slowed my pace. What Isabel said outside began to sink in, settling in my core like molten rock.

I stopped, turning toward her. "I started this, didn't I?"

Isabel sighed and put her hand on my arm. The connection produced a cold spot where her hand landed and I shivered in response.

"I don't know. You shouldn't be seeing us just yet, so I don't have the answers for you. All I know is those reapers are badass. They've wanted to see the destruction of mankind for millennia now."

A throat cleared, and I spun toward the noise. Julia stood a few feet from us with her hand on her hip and when her gaze met mine, it was full of that jealous rage I've seen before when she caught me flirting with a couple of the cheerleaders after a football game. "Who's this?"

I had to come up with an answer, and fast.

"I'm Isabel Ramsay, Nick's cousin," Isabel said before I could conjure up a reasonable answer. I gave her a sideways glance. Her use of my father's surname created a jolt of energy in my chest, and I wondered if it was just a coincidence.

Julia glanced at me, her brow knit in an unspoken question.

"Yeah, I didn't know I had cousins either," I said, adding another layer to the lie.

"Oh," Julia said, and offered an embarrassed smile. She stuck out her hand. "I'm Julia."

Isabel stared at her hand and then glanced at me.

"Izzy has a weird allergy to people," I said, and pushed Julia's hand down. "Just touching someone can trigger hives. It's gross," I added just for effect.

Julia stuffed her hands in her pockets and shifted from one foot to the other. "You were gone so long I got worried."

"I'm sorry I took so long," I said, and glanced over her shoulder at the table I left her at. The books were still spread out like when I left. "Did you get your homework done?"

"Pretty much."

"Then let's pack up so we can get out of here."

"What about your book report?"

I glanced at Julia and shrugged. "I'll do it later. Izzy wants to visit for a while, so..." I didn't know what else to say and just trailed off. I needed to talk to Izzy, and having Julia around today was going to be a royal pain.

"Okay, just give me a minute." Julia flashed the smile that always made me forget where I was, then she turned and headed toward the table to collect her books. I stared after her, watching the sway of her hips.

"She's cute."

"I know." I pulled my gaze from Julia and glanced at Isabel. "Is your last name really Ramsay?"

She smiled.

"We're related?"

"Yes."

"How?"

"Royal bloodline." She nodded toward Julia. "I'll explain later."

"Ready?" Julia asked and slung her backpack over her shoulder.

"Sure."

The walk home became increasingly uncomfortable with starts and stops of conversations and Julia's awkward questions about the family. I left Isabel on our doorstep and walked Julia home.

"Isabel is a little strange, don't you think?" Julia whispered as we crossed the yard.

I couldn't help but smile. "It seems the entire family on my father's side is a bit strange."

She giggled and when she stepped onto her porch, she glanced at my house and the smile faded. "I saw you talking to her outside the library and at first I thought you were into her..."

"Julia, I'm with you." I pulled her into a hug, trying to put her fears at ease. Julia really did not know how far gone I was for her. I'd walk through the fires of Hell just to be with her and there wasn't anything I wouldn't do to keep her safe.

Unfortunately, I had a feeling the reapers knew that, too.

CHAPTER 15

ISABEL TOOK A seat on the couch after wandering around the living room, enamored with the knick-knacks my mother had on the end tables and the little shelves peppered on the walls. "Your mother and I met once." She sighed, meeting my gaze.

"How are we related?"

"I'm your father's great-great grandmother."

My legs suddenly felt like liquid and I collapsed on the couch. That meant she was four generations older than me and yet she only looked a couple of years older.

"I'm not as old as those other reapers, but you're right. I'm much older than this form I took." She looked out the window. "I've been a reaper for over two hundred years."

I blinked, staring at the carpet in front of me, and then my gaze snapped in her direction. "If you've been a reaper that long, how did you meet my mother?"

"Your mother had a close call once, and I was dispatched."

"You mean my mother almost died?"

"Yes," she said, but didn't elaborate.

"Was she supposed to die?"

Isabel inhaled, and she looked away from me. The silence settled over the room like a suffocating blanket.

"Was she?"

"Not exactly," Isabel said. "It all depended upon your father and the choices he had to make."

"What the Hell are you talking about?"

"There is a choice, but not a palatable one and there has never been an ancestor of the royal bloodline that has chosen the alternative," Isabel explained. "You will be put in the same position when the time comes."

I stared at her, my mind whirling with the facts, and the conversation with my father surfaced. "He said there was no choice." Even as the words spilled out, I got it. His choice was clear-his life, his future, for ours.

"Did he really die on September 11th?" I asked, thinking about the facts my mother told me.

"Yes, and you and your mother were there that day."

I raised my eyebrows. I was two at the time and had no recollection of that day at all. My mom said she watched the news from our apartment while I played with the toy fire trucks my father had given me. Why wouldn't she tell me we were there?

"She has no memory of the events, Nicholas. We erased the horror of that day, replacing it with what she believes is the truth."

"What about my memory?"

"You don't have one because you died in your father's arms."

Sounds swirled, taking over the silence of the living room. Thunder and screaming, dust and blood rained over my world and my breath hitched. In the rubble kneeled a firefighter, his face covered with grit and tears, and in his arms the broken body of a small boy. His gaze rose to mine and shock saturated my body at the familiar blue-green glow that stood out against the soot.

"Nick?"

It wasn't so much her voice that brought me back to the present. It was the icy touch on my arm and I blinked the disturbing vision away and looked at Isabel.

"He traded his life for mine, didn't he?" The weight of his sacrifice crumbled any resolve I had and tears blurred my vision.

"Yes, he did. Just like his father did before him, but your father tempted Fate and ignore his destiny before making that decision."

"Why?"

"Because he wanted a life with you and your mother as opposed to taking the role of the Angel of Death that his royal bloodline demanded. Your father didn't believe your grandfather's ultimatum. He ignored the responsibility, and the ramifications of his ignorance rippled through the underworld. September 11th resulted from that decision and they presented your father with one last option. Take the position or the bloodline would be severed, plunging the world into anarchy."

"If I was already dead..."

"Not only does Death have the power to take life, he has the power to breathe it back into the dead. He revived you and your mother and made sure neither of you had any recollection of that day."

"How did he die?"

"The minute we cleared you from the building, the section he was in collapsed under the weight of the debris, crushing your father."

"Were we the only ones he saved that day?"

Isabel smiled and shook her head. "No. He saved several people before he died and after he took his rightful place as the Angel of Death, he shepherded those not on the list to safety."

"If he erased our memories, how did my mom know about him?"

"Your parent discussed your father's future before you were born. He told her about his lineage and that he had a choice and he wanted to stay with the two of you. Of course, she thought the entire thing was his overactive imagination until the night of September 11th, when the torch was passed and he violated all the rules by going home and explaining the crux of the responsibility. This birthright is passed from generation to generation and someday you would stand in his shoes. She begged him not to go until he told her it was his life or yours. While your mother loved your father with every fiber of her being, she loves you more. He broke protocol explaining everything to your mother. No other living human knows about the royal bloodline or the fact that it is passed on from generation to generation, and she made him promise to explain it to you long before you had to make the same grave choices.”

“She doesn't know I died.”

“No. She doesn't, but she knows you will when it's time to take your father's place.

CHAPTER 16

EVERY WORD ISABEL said echoed in my mind with each sway of the front porch swing, swarming and overwhelming me, until I closed my eyes. Every time I closed my eyes, I saw that snapshot of my father holding my dead body, and raw devastation slammed into my ribs like right hooks, forcing my eyelids open. This vicious cycle looped again and again, as lazy as the arch of the swing but as powerful as a gale force wind.

I sucked in my breath against the mental anguish.

I wouldn't live beyond twenty-five. Half my life was already gone and that little fact stroked my nerves like a sharp knife tearing flesh from bone.

A Death sentence of epic proportion.

At least with cancer, there was a fighting chance, but this? This was a time bomb I didn't want to hold. My gaze landed on Julia's house and my prospects for the future darkened.

A car engine drew my attention, and I turned toward the driveway. My mother climbed out of the car with a grocery bag in her arms and her warm welcoming smile. My throat closed tight at the onslaught of sorrow and I pressed my lips together, blinking the tears blurring my vision.

My mom's smile faded the closer she got, and I tilted my head, opting to stare at the wooden deck instead of at her.

The bag crinkled when she set it down near the door and her feet came into my field of view. "What's wrong, Nick?" she asked and kneeled so I could see her face.

Before I could answer, a deep rumble came from below us, shaking the porch. A plume of fire rolled into the air in the distance like the cloud of a nuclear bomb and the noise that followed sounded like the earth screaming.

The wind roared; bending the trees in its path until the scorching breeze dissipated.

Both my mother and I jumped to our feet. Neighbors' doors opened and folks just stood and stared at the settling smoke.

"What the Hell was that?" my mother said.

"It's started," Isabel said from the edge of the porch stairs, yanking our attention away from the spectacle.

"Who are you?"

I knew that accusatory tone my mother uttered. It was her defense mechanism when she was rattled and her weapon when she was angry.

"Isabel." She took a step forward. "Nick and I met at the hospital earlier today."

It was my turn to get the sharp stare, and I fidgeted. "I thought you were going to the library with Julia."

"I did, but then I went to the hospital to look for reapers and I found Isabel." I waved my hand toward the pretty teenager on the steps.

My mother's face paled, and she took a seat on the swing, studying Isabel. "Are you..."

"Yes. I am."

I started to speak, but a quick shake from Isabel's head shut off my words.

"Why can I see you?"

Isabel sighed and glanced toward the growing mayhem of sirens in the distance. "I'm related to Dylan," she said when she looked back at my mother.

The muscles in my mother's jaw tightened, and she crossed her arms. "Part of that royal bloodline?" Sarcasm laced each syllable.

"Married to it.," Isabel said.

My mother's arms dropped to her lap and her mouth popped open in an O of surprise.

"Not Dylan. No honey, you've got his heart forever. I was married to his great-great-grandfather. This is what happens when we die, darling. We serve the bloodline."

A crease appeared between my mother's eyes and I could see the wheels turning in her head as she stared at Isabel. A pack of questions circled in her mind like a dog chasing its tail and I had to look away. My gaze traveled toward Julia's house and I blinked. Julia was in full sprint towards us, her face flushed and her eyes wild.

I hopped over the rail and sprinted toward her.

"Nick," she said, her breath laboring around my name.

"What's wrong?" I asked, knowing how dumb the question was considering the number of sirens in the distance.

"I was on the phone with my mom. She said she and my dad were going to be late because of the traffic on the highway and then the phone died."

"Maybe..."

"Nick, the phone died at the same time that explosion happened." She threw herself into my chest.

I wrapped my arms around her trembling body and stared at the settling dust in the distance. To say I had a bad feeling was an understatement.

CHAPTER 17

JULIA SAT STARING at the television, her milk and cookies untouched. The news station rattled on about a gas tanker that exploded on the crowded highway, but there was no footage being broadcast and only speculation regarding the amount of damage.

She turned her teary gaze in my direction, silently pleading for information that I didn't have. Isabel had left soon after we brought Julia in the house and she sent me a clear warning to stay put.

That had been at least a half hour ago and I was getting tired of waiting. "Mom, I'm going to take my dirt bike and find out what happened."

"No."

There was no wiggle room in her answer, or in the glare she shot over Julia's head.

"I need to know what happened," I said, a little more forcefully than I meant, causing darkness to cross over my mother's face, transitioning it from worry to anger in the matter of a blink.

"Dylan Nicholas Ramsay, you are not going anywhere. You understand?"

Julia stiffened and her hand clasping mine clamped down with enough force for me to wince and snap my attention to where hers was glued. The first footage of the wreckage scrolled across the television and it looked like a war zone. Charred metal and fabric and other unidentifiable remains splattered both sides of the highway, and the area where the gas truck had been was now a smoldering blackened crater.

"Maybe they were still on the bridge," I said, trying to instill hope where I knew there was none.

The reapers caused this atrocity. Those people, Julia's parents included, were not supposed to die today and my free hand balled into a fist. My fingernails dug into my palm, tempering my building fury. Julia needed me to be reasonable and calm, not go off half-cocked and get myself killed.

The shrill ring of the phone made us jump and my mother picked it up.

"Hello?" After the flutter of words on the other end, she turned away. "I see," her voice hitched. "Thank you for taking care of her the last couple of days. I'll contact the funeral home and make arrangements."

Both Julia and I were staring at my mother when she hung up the phone. When she turned, her eyes were bloodshot and full of unshed tears. "Nick, your grandmother passed away."

"Do you think my father...?" I trailed off, and a voice cleared from the hallway.

Isabel stood in the shadows, and her gaze told me all I needed to know. She was the one who fixed my mistake, not my father. And I could tell from the sadness in her eyes that she couldn't fix the chain of devastation the rogue reapers had started.

"Isabel," my mother's cool voice pulled my attention back to the situation. "What did you find out?"

Isabel's gaze bounced between the three of us, and her features etched with indecision.

Julia turned toward Isabel and sniffed, wiping the tear tracks from her cheeks and waiting for the axe to fall on her world.

"I'm sorry, Julia," Isabel whispered.

"What does that mean?" Julia asked, her gaze falling on me.

"It means your parents didn't make it," I said, steeling myself for a storm of emotion.

"How do you know that? *They* don't even know that yet." She pointed at the television. "They said it could take days to sort through the wreckage and figure out how many were lost in the explosion."

"Look, she's in just as much danger as you and your mother right now and she deserves to know what I am, so we might as well come clean," Isabel said.

I tightened my jaw and glared at Isabel while Julia fell silent. She turned her pretty doe eyes in my direction. "What does she mean?"

My mother opened her mouth to speak, and I silenced her with the same motion my father had last night. "I got this, Mom." I met Julia's gaze. "Do you remember me yelling when Mr. Sanchez died?"

She nodded.

"Well, I saw something behind him." I paused and traded a glance with Isabel. "I saw a reaper."

"No one was in the room, Nick," she said.

"Normal people can't see reapers, but I can."

"Look, your cousin just told me my parents are dead and all you can talk about are things only you can see?" Her voice rose to a hysterical pitch and her chest rose and fell with the effort. Tears slid down her cheeks and I reached for her, but she pulled away. "You're insane!"

I grabbed her arm, holding her close. "You said my father scared you

124

and that Isabel was a little strange," I started, trying not to let the swell of emotion take over, but my voice shook regardless of how much I wanted to sound in control. "You knew they weren't normal."

"What does that have to do with reapers?"

"Isabel *is* a reaper."

The admission dropped her jaw and her eyes widened like saucers. I didn't expect her next reaction and when the sting of her palm slapped my cheek, I stepped back, dropping my hold from her and covering the hot skin of my face.

"Izzy, show her," I ordered, and both my mother's and Julia's gasp were enough. I didn't have to turn to know Isabel transitioned into her natural form, allowing Julia to see her without her glamor. Julia moved quickly, clinging to me like a frightened two-year-old.

"What is that?"

I glanced over my shoulder and shrugged at the cloaked skeleton. "Thanks Isabel, now can you..." Before I finished the sentence, the perky teenage girl again stood in the same spot and I turned back to Julia. "That is a reaper."

Julia's eyes rolled back, and she went limp in my arms.

CHAPTER 18

I DON'T KNOW how to stop this," Isabel whispered and for the first time, I sensed her fear. I glanced over my shoulder at Julia on the couch, still in the black out zone and my mother mopping Julia's forehead with a damp washcloth. I nodded toward the living room and Isabel led the way.

"Can I stop it?"

She shook her head and then bit her lip.

"You don't know whether I can or not, do you?"

Isabel paced the floor without answering me.

"Can my father stop this?"

She stopped pacing and met my gaze. "I don't know."

"Okay, let me ask you a different question." I leaned forward. "How do I kill a reaper?"

She recoiled, her arms wrapping around her chest in response to the fear I instilled in her. Just the thought made her shiver. This time when she whispered, "I don't know," I knew she was lying.

"Tell me how to kill a reaper," I commanded in a voice I didn't recognize.

Isabel shuddered and then the explanation came in a rush of words, spilled too fast for me to understand. The only thing I got was a blade and a foreign alloy.

"Dylan usually has the weapon," she finished.

"What kind of weapon?" I asked, thinking it was the traditional scythe shown in the Google searches.

"It's a fifteen-inch spiked bowie knife."

"Can't we buy one online?"

Isabel laughed at me and the burn of embarrassment heated my cheeks. "No, you can't just buy it online. It isn't made of anything you'd find on this earth. The archangels delivered it to the first Angel of Death and it's been handed down from generation to generation ever since. It can destroy many things, including reapers, and possession of that weapon wields ultimate power."

I raised my eyebrow. "What if my father doesn't have it anymore?"

Isabel blanched and sat down on the couch. "If those reapers have that knife, humanity is doomed."

CHAPTER 19

THE TELEVISION WAS still droning about the explosion when I stepped back into the family room. Julia sobbed in my mother's arms and my heart dropped to my stomach, wrapping me in the pain she felt. I crossed and dropped to my knees next to her. I reached for her, and when my hand touched her knee, she jumped, jerking away from both my mother and me.

Her eyes darted around the room, searching for Isabel.

"She went to look for something," I said to ease her panic, and it worked. Her teary gaze met mine and her chin quivered. I took this as my cue and pulled her into my arms. "I'm sorry about your parents," I whispered in her ear and shut everything else from my mind. Julia needed me and I owed it to her to be there.

When she stopped shaking, she pulled away and wiped her face with a Kleenex. "Why is Isabel here?"

"She's trying to help," I said.

"Nick," my mother said, shooting the same warning look she gave me before she left me in Father Michael's office.

"Mom, she deserves to know," I said, and did something I would never have dreamed of doing twenty-four hours ago. I glared at my mother. "She deserves the choice you never had."

My mother's lips thinned, and she stood. "I wouldn't change a thing."

"You mean to tell me if you knew what you were getting into, what you were bringing me into, you still would have married him?"

"Yes." The answer came without a blink of hesitation.

I didn't care. Julia deserved more.

I turned away from my mother. "The way I understand it, I will not live beyond twenty-five and when I die, I take over my father's job."

Julia pulled out of my arms and stepped back, putting distance between us. "Why are you doing this?"

"I'm not doing anything, Julia. I'm just trying to tell you who I am."

"I already know who you are."

"Do you know who my father is?" I didn't mean to, but my voice rose under the stress racking my bones. "He scared the crap out of you, Julia. Tell me who you thought he was?"

"Nick, don't…"

I swiveled my gaze to my mother, and she stopped. "Tell her who my father is."

My mother didn't answer fast enough, and I turned back to Julia. "My father is Death in the flesh." The absence of noise that followed reminded me of how the air stilled before a big thunderstorm and the room even flashed that funky green hue for a moment in my mind's eye.

Julia's mouth hung open, and she just stared in silence, her gaze jumping from me to my mother and back. My mother studied the floor, unable to meet her fluttering gaze, and she turned, leaving Julia and I alone in the room to work this out.

My aggravation melted away with the purge of the truth and I sighed. "Are you going to say something?"

"Your father's responsible for my parents' Death?"

I should have guessed that's where her mind would land, and I shook my head. "No. My father's been kidnapped."

Surprise layered over the grief and a crease appeared between her eyes. With a cock of her head, she repeated the word like she tasted something sour. "Kidnapped?"

"Yes. And a few rogue reapers have waged war. That's why your parents died."

"Why? What does that have to do with the explosion on the highway?"

"Because my father was trying to fix a mistake I made, and the reapers didn't want him to. So, if you want to get technical on me, all those people died because I ordered the reaper taking my grandmother to stop. That's what started this and now I've got to figure out how to stop them before they destroy our world."

CHAPTER 20

I LAY IN bed and stared into the darkness, my head pounding in time with my heartbeat, and I wondered how Julia was sleeping. She cut me off after my disastrous explanation this afternoon, and I didn't broach the subject again. Dinner was excruciating, with only the scraping of silverware against the dishes as conversation, and

Julia headed to the guest room right after we ate.

Isabel hadn't returned from wherever she disappeared to, so it left me channel surfing while my mother consoled Julia. And now I couldn't sleep.

"Nick, are you awake?" Julia's voice penetrated the dark and the creak of my door followed.

"Yeah."

"I can't sleep." The door clicked closed, and I heard her shuffling in the dark toward the bed.

"Neither can I." I waited. When the bed creaked with her weight, I sat up and reached in the dark. My hand landed on her arm and I pulled her closer. I knew if my mother caught us together, we'd get in trouble, but at the moment, I really didn't care.

Julia scooted next to me and snuggled into my shoulder as we leaned against the headboard. "I'm sorry I freaked out on you earlier."

"Don't worry about it." I planted a kiss on her forehead. "You've had a bad day."

She chuckled. "Ya think?"

I could almost see her sarcastic smile in the dark. This was one of the reasons I loved Julia. Her sense of humor was epic. Twisted, but epic.

"I don't know what's going to happen to me now."

"You can stay with us," I said, not knowing if that really was the case, but at least she could stay until they figured out what to do. Her only relative lived far enough away to make me not want to even consider the alternative.

"I'm not sure I can. It depends on whether my aunt will want me with her in Florida or not."

I didn't acknowledge her statement, but my stomach plunged at the thought and I tightened my grip around her.

"I don't want to leave either."

Silence settled between us and I couldn't help thinking about Fate. Was this part of her game? Smashing my future just because I made a mistake? If it was, I'd have a word or two to say to that fickle bitch.

"And what would those words be?"

My muscles contracted, and Julia stiffened in my arms. I reached and flipped on my light, the sight before us pulled a gasp from both our lips.

A woman, more beautiful than any supermodel I've ever seen, stood at the end of the bed dressed in a blood red gown that seemed to flow in a perpetual breeze. Her eyes looked like golden saucers, sparkling with a humorless glow.

Julia pushed into me, trying to get as close as possible. If she could have jumped into my skin, I think she would have. "Who is that?" she whispered.

"That is Fate," I answered and received a nod from the apparition.

"And you called me a bitch."

I allowed a smile and a shrug. In the context of my thoughts, it was entirely appropriate.

"I don't like being called a bitch for no reason, especially from the brat that started this mess."

"I didn't know this would happen." A lame excuse if I've ever heard one, but true nonetheless.

"Where is your father?"

I stared at her and clamped down on my thoughts on instinct. "You don't know?"

"Don't toy with me. Where is he?"

She didn't know, and that realization gave me the unwelcomed sensation of being skinned alive. I swallowed and weighed my options. Julia still clung to me, shifting to use me as a buffer between her and the crazy lady at the end of my bed. I didn't know what the truth would spawn, but maybe it would put Fate on our side.

"The reapers that caused the highway explosion kidnapped my father."

The perpetual wind calmed, and Fate raised her eyebrows. "So, you're telling me he isn't behind this slight?"

"No, he's not."

Fate moved closer and took a seat at the end of my bed. Instinctively, both Julia and I pulled our legs up. I peered over my knees at the confusion on Fate's face. Her scrunched eyebrows smoothed and the muscles in her jaw tensed. She swung her blazing gaze in my direction. "There's nothing I hate more than reapers gone rogue."

I couldn't disagree with her, but her tone held me accountable, and I shifted, wondering if testing her with a glib response was a smart thing. I clamped my lips closed against any retort and glanced at Julia. "They killed her parents."

"I'm aware of who died today," she snapped. "But this was not planned, and you need to stop it. Now. Before I lose my patience."

"I'm trying."

"Try harder because if any more unplanned deaths occur, I'm holding you responsible." With that, she stood and dissolved in a swirl of red steam.

"Fate's a real person?"

Julia's question pushed a button deep in my soul, and I chuckled. I couldn't help it. The lunacy of the entire situation struck me and the chortle transitioned into a full out belly laugh.

"Nick, shush, your mother is going to hear you."

She was right, of course, but I couldn't stop, even when the muscles in my belly protested. I clamped my hands over my mouth to muffle the noise and, through tear-blurred eyes, I met Julia's gaze. At least she was smiling, but underneath the dimples, I saw the sorrow filling her. It was sobering, and my laughter wound down. "I'm sorry, I just couldn't help it," I whispered when I had control of all my faculties. "Looks like Fate is as real as Death."

Julia sighed and nodded. She dropped her gaze to her hands and started picking at a hangnail. "So, someday you'll be Death?"

"Yeah, that seems to be the plan unless the world ends."

"What if I don't want you to?"

I thought about my father and the choice that was made for him. "It doesn't matter what you want or what I want. It's just the way it has to be."

"Why?"

"Because if I choose not to take the job, everything we know and love will be destroyed." That was the only way I knew how to get her to understand. There was no choice for me. There only was a choice for her. "So, the choice really is yours. I know we're only thirteen and who knows if we'll even be together when I turn twenty-five, but right now, I can't see me trusting anyone else with this. And as I said earlier, you deserve to know what you're getting into if you stay." I held my breath, praying she wouldn't opt out, but if I were in her shoes, I'd be running as far away as I could from this freaky situation.

But Julia wasn't me, and she straightened her back and her chin jutted out in that stubborn resolve. "I'm not going anywhere. I want to see those reapers that killed my parents destroyed."

CHAPTER 21

I WOKE SPOONING Julia, and I gasped at the sight of sunlight streaming through the window. "Jules," I whispered and shook her. She rolled toward me and then her eyes shot to the window and the bright blue sky.

She moved quickly, jumping out of bed in an all-out sprint, and before I could say anything else, she was out in the hallway and out of sight.

I flopped back on the bed and glanced at the clock. Thank God it was Sunday and not a weekday, because my mother slept in on Sundays. If it had been during the week, we would have been so busted.

I had another hour before I expected my mother to pop into my room and wake me for church. As much as I grumbled at getting up at seven-thirty, my religious duties were over by ten and I had the rest of the day to do whatever I wanted.

I rolled toward the window and stared at the cloud-free sky, and the deception of a calm spring day, when I knew the Storm of the Century was just around the bend. A scraping noise filled the room, and I sat up, my eyes darting from corner to corner and then they fell to the floor and my eyes widened.

A reaper half crawled, half dragged itself toward me, and I scrambled to the headboard, unable to make a sound. The thing was missing a leg and one arm was bent at an unnatural angle, held together by splinters of bone. Its good arm reached for me and I heard the familiar voice in my head.

"Nicholas..."

I moved on instinct, reaching for Isabel's skeletal hand and the moment my flesh touched her, the information flowed in a flurry of facts and visions, none of which settled my unease. "What happened?" I asked, because I didn't trust what I saw in my head.

"Leviathan," she gasped.

"You went to Purgatory?" I already knew the answer, but I just couldn't believe she'd do something so stupid.

"Had to try, but I couldn't get to your father."

Once I had her settled on the bed, I sat next to her and rested my hand on her shoulder. The chill I felt from her yesterday was gone. A dull sense of pain replaced it with an aching in my chest and I couldn't place why. "So, did he have the knife?"

"No, he doesn't have it," she said, her voice getting weaker with every word, and I knew.

Sadness filled me and I knew Isabel was dying.

"I thought only the knife could kill reapers," I said, trying to make sense of this.

"Leviathan. Can kill. Us," Isabel said, and each word captured the pain and desperation filling both of us.

"I'm sorry, Izzy." Tears stung my eyes and burned my throat and I pressed my lips together in protest against the devastation welling in my throat.

She reached her bony hand to my cheek, wiping the tear away before her arm fell to the bed. "Your. Father. Hid. The..." The last word came as an exhale and then nothing else.

"Isabel!" I yelled.

Nothing but a hiss of wind against my window broke the silence, and I stared at the form on my bed, watching helplessly as her bones turned to a fine powder that swirled away in the turbulent dust tornado.

I turned toward the door in time to see both Julia and my mother slide to a stop in the entrance.

"What's wrong?" they asked in unison.

"Isabel is dead."

Both of them blinked in confusion, trading a glance before looking back at me.

"She's a reaper," my mother started.

"Yes, and she got really hurt going after my father. She came back." I stopped and swallowed, trying to figure out the right words to articulate the shape she was in. "Broken," I added.

"What do you mean, broken?" Julia asked, stepping inside the room, her eyes darting around, expecting to see the glamor Isabel wore for her benefit. The empty room greeted her with every glance.

"Her leg was torn off, her arm was broken, and it looked like a few ribs were crushed. She said Leviathan did it."

My mom reached for the desk chair and sat down hard. "Did she say anything about your father?"

"Dad's alive," I said to her devastated face. "Well, as alive as Death can be."

"Did Isabel find what she was looking for?" Julia asked, trying to keep our conversation regarding the magical knife under wraps, but needing some answer that would revive her hope.

"She found my dad, but she couldn't get him away from the Leviathan," I said, conveying the no in so many words and her shoulders slumped.

My mother glanced between us and cocked her head. "What exactly was Isabel looking for?" I swear, the woman could read minds as easily as I would be able to when I stepped into my father's job.

"She was looking for my father," I answered and looked at the floorboards. I hated lying to my mother, and like a search and rescue dog—she ferreted out the lie.

"Dylan Nicholas Ramsay," she started, and I met her gaze.

"Mom, leave it alone."

"I will do no such thing." She stood, putting her hands on her hips in that exasperated manner that always made me want to laugh.

I crossed my arms and stared her down, unwilling to share this little tidbit of information.

"You're not leaving this room until you tell me what Isabel was looking for."

"She was looking for Death's dagger," Julia said.

My jaw dropped. "It's not a dagger," I corrected and sent a just shut up now look in her direction.

"Why?"

"Because Isabel told Nick it can kill the reapers," Julia answered.

My mother's eyebrows rose, and she glanced at Julia for a moment before returning her eagle-eyed glare in my direction. "And you thought if you found this weapon, you could stop this?"

I nodded. "I have to stop them, Mom."

"Don't be stupid, Nick, you're not equipped to take on a reaper, never mind two hell bent on killing all of us."

"If that knife gets into the wrong hands, it won't matter," I said.

My mother's arms slowly lowered, and she sat in the chair again.

"Isabel said my father hid it somewhere. I have to find it before they do." I studied her reaction, or lack of one, and my intuition prickled. "Did you ever see my father with a knife?"

She glanced out the window and nodded.

"When?"

Her gaze met mine, and I shivered. He had it the last time he was here.

"You know where it is?"

Her gaze was the tell, and I felt both cold and hot flush over me. I slid off the bed and stuck my hands between the mattresses, sliding it along the length of my bed.

"Nick, don't," my mother pleaded, but I ignored her.

When my fingers hit cool leather, I felt along the sheath until the smooth hilt caressed my fingertips. Carefully, I wrapped my hand around the handle and pulled. The minute the knife hit the air of my room, an icy wind filled the space and I glanced at my mother's wide eyes.

Power radiated through the sheath, producing a glow that flowed out over the handle. I unsnapped the clasps holding the knife in place, freeing the blade from the leather holder. The room lit up as if I was holding Excalibur instead of a fifteen-inch spiked bowie knife. It pulsed in my hand, sending warm radiating waves up my arms and filling me with a sense of invincibility.

I yanked my gaze from the blade and met Julia's. Her mouth formed a perfect O, and I smiled. I'm sure I must look like an idiot holding the knife like a revered object, but I didn't care. With this, I could do anything. Even defeat the rogue reapers.

I slid the knife back in the sheath and clipped it onto my pajama bottoms. It pulled at the fabric, lowering the flannel below my belly button, and I clutched the waistband with a shrug. "I guess pajama bottoms aren't the best thing to clip this on. Do you mind giving me a minute so I can get dressed?"

They both nodded and slipped out of the room. On instinct, I didn't put the sheath down. Instead, I slipped it between my teeth and once I had a clean pair of jeans on; I clipped the sheath to my belt. Warmth radiated through the leather and into my hip, creating a dull ache, like it wanted to be freed from its bondage to wield justice. I patted the holder, calming the instinctual need for vengeance.

A flannel shirt took the chill from my skin, even though I left it unbuttoned, and I made my way downstairs into the kitchen. When I stepped across the threshold, Julia slid into a seat at the kitchen table with two bowls and the box of Captain Crunch from the cupboard.

"Want to grab the milk and some spoons?"

"Sure, where's my mom?"

"She said she needed to get ready for church."

"Did you want to come to church with us?"

Julia shook her head. And I couldn't blame her.

"Do you want me to stay here with you?" I asked, and she hesitated with the cereal box half tilted and without saying a word, she nodded and continued to fill both our bowls. I sat down next to her and handed her one of the spoons before drowning both bowls in milk.

We ate in silence, but I picked up more than a hint of her thoughts and I wondered if the knife had something to do with my heightened senses. She waffled on whether to check her house. The police might have left a message or some sort of notice to contact them, assuming they had some way to identify bodies this quickly, or at least identify license plates in the charred wreckage.

With the onset of those morbid thoughts, my appetite vanished. I pushed the bowl away half-eaten and wiped my face with my hands before glancing sideways at her. It didn't seem to spoil her appetite, and she even opted for more. I stood, clearing my dish and dumping and stashing it in the dishwasher before I turned.

"I can go with you to your house to get your school books and clothes for tomorrow if you want."

She raised her head and her gaze fell on the knife attached to my hip and she nodded, dropping her gaze again. Her not saying anything beyond two sentences since I found the knife worried me. "Is everything okay?"

This time, she looked directly at me and raised an eyebrow. "Have you looked in the mirror since you got a hold of that thing?"

A bite of shock traversed over my skin and for a moment I wasn't looking at her, but looking through her eyes, and what I saw sent me running to the bathroom. I stared at my reflection. My normal reflection with my hair in bedhead mode, my shirt still hanging unbuttoned and none of what I saw through her eyes.

Even Halloween wouldn't explain the red and black face painting that looked like tiger stripes and add the bizarre ninja suit, and you could mistake me as an extra from The Phantom Menace. The only thing remotely familiar was the sheath on my hip.

I started laughing and my mother pushed open the door. She did a double take and her lips pressed together. "Why are you dressed like Superman?"

"I'm not."

She huffed at me and then blinked, the crease between her eyes becoming more pronounced as she studied me.

She did a quick shake of her head and then laughed. "I could have sworn..."

"Yeah, well, you should have seen me through Julia's eyes." I took another quick look in the mirror. I was still the same me I expected to see, and I shrugged, offering my mother a smile as I squeaked by her.

"You need to get ready for church," she said as I stepped away.

I stopped and turned toward her. "Julia doesn't want to go, and I don't want to leave her alone."

She scowled and looked toward the kitchen. I could tell she was weighing her options. Leaving us alone in the house together wasn't something she was used to doing, but she needed to go to the church and talk with Father Michael about funeral arrangements. I could see the decision coming and I headed her off.

"Julia doesn't want to go to her house alone. I told her I'd go with her while she checks the answering machine and gets her school stuff." I knew it was a slim chance, but I had to try.

"I don't know, Nick."

"I promise we'll be good. We'll just go to her house and come back, okay?"

She sighed and closed her eyes. Not usually a good sign, but this time, she just nodded and walked away.

"Mom?"

She turned and waited.

"Are you okay?"

She sent me a smile, but the sudden gloss over her eyes told me more than words could. I crossed and gave her a hug and she held me tight, giving me one final squeeze before she turned and slipped into her room, closing the door. The wood barrier didn't silence that first sob, but the rest remained unvoiced, and I turned away before the tears burning my throat surfaced.

CHAPTER 22

I SAT IN the family room, surfing the channels on the television while Julia cleaned up. There were no messages on the answering machine or the cell phone and I wondered if we should call the police and report her parents missing, but Julia shot down the suggestion. I think she was hoping for a miracle—one we both knew was impossible.

The burning on my hip stepped up a notch, and I glanced at the knife. A red hue flowed from the sheath, and I stood, unsnapping the leather strap holding it in place. Wrapping my fingers around the hilt sent hot shivers up my arm like a subliminal warning and I bolted for the stairs, taking them two at a time with my heart pulsing in my throat.

I burst into Julia's bedroom with the knife in hand, my eyes darting from her half-dressed form to the far corner where a reaper stood. Julia couldn't see it, but his sinister smile told me more than words could. This wasn't a friendly reaper, and it was here for my girlfriend.

"Nick!" Julia covered her exposed bra with a shirt.

I hardly noticed. Instead, I moved, intercepting its path and blocking it from getting to Julia.

"You think you can stop me, boy?" the reaper snarled.

"Try me." I tightened my grip on the knife and shifted so my body turned to the side. I brought the blade to my waist, ready to strike if the thing moved toward us. I just hoped like Hell I knew where to hit the thing to destroy it, because, otherwise, all it would do would piss it off.

"What are you doing?" Julia said from behind me.

"Just stay behind me," I said, without taking my eyes off the advancing reaper. Judging distance was never my strong suit in martial arts class, and I took a deep breath, waiting until I was sure it was within the kill zone.

The reaper hesitated, and I narrowed my eyes, waving it in with a smile of my own. "Looks like I'm not the one who's chicken," I taunted.

That did the trick. The thing launched toward me and I stepped forward in a lunge thrust, jabbing the blade through the black cloak where I thought the human heart would be. A scream shattered the room and ice flowed up my arm into my shoulder. I twisted the knife and winced at the high-pitched wail, but I didn't pull away. Instead, I let the anger boiling in my blood take control and I twisted and slashed until the reaper exploded in a cloud of dust.

I stood in the maelstrom of mist with my chest heaving and a dull ache in the muscles of my right arm. When the wind surrounding me died down, I glanced at the knife in my hand. It no longer glowed or vibrated in warning and I slipped it back into the sheath. I took a deep breath, aware of Julia's raspy wheeze behind me, and turned to meet her wide-eyed gaze.

"You okay?" I asked and stepped toward her.

She backed into the wall, answering my question without as much as a peep.

The fear radiated from her like gamma waves, prickling my nerves and for a moment, I saw through her eyes and I wasn't a ninja like earlier. This time what she saw me as sent a shiver of revulsion down my spine.

A cloaked skeleton with sharp shark's teeth reached for her.

I pulled my hand back, knowing it would do no good to reach out to her. Not with her seeing me like that, so I stepped back, putting distance between us. "Julia, it's okay. It's me, Nick." I took another stride backward.

Her face reddened. "I saw it kill you!"

"Close your eyes, Julia. Concentrate on my voice," I said, taming the panic throbbing in my temples, but she just shook her head, her gaze tracking me like a frightened child. "Please. I promise I won't hurt you." I put my palms facing her and prayed she'd listen. I needed her to clear her mind, to concentrate on me. "Please," I whispered.

She must have heard the plea in my voice because she closed her eyes, squeezing tears out of the corners, and I watched the slow track down her cheeks and focused on her quivering chin, swallowing the lump in my throat before I spoke. "Can you hear me?"

She nodded.

"Do you believe it's really me?"

Hesitation and my heart sank.

"It's me, Julia. There was a reaper in your room when I came in and I got it, not the other way around." I swept my fingers through my hair. "Isabel was right - the knife *can* kill a reaper."

Her eyelids popped open, and she stared at me, her chin quivering before she flew across the space. I wrapped my arms around her trembling form and held her, thanking God for small favors.

"I thought it killed you," she said against my shoulder.

"Nah, not even a scratch." I kissed her cheek.

She pulled away from my grasp and ran her fingers down my cheek. "Why am I seeing these things?"

"I don't know." I met her gaze. "I think the knife feeds off your imagination somehow."

Her exposed skin puckered into a landscape of bumps and she rubbed her arms. "That's just freaky."

I let out a laugh, and she smacked my arm.

"Don't laugh at me."

"I'm not laughing at you. I'm just laughing at the whole situation. I've got the strongest weapon on earth and when I take it out of its sheath, people around me start seeing things."

"Kind of like the glamor spells in Harry Potter."

I raised an eyebrow at the thought. "I wonder if you're creating images based on my emotions."

A crease appeared between her pretty brown eyes. "What do you mean?"

"I'm not sure. All I know is I was scared out of my wits when I first ran in here, and earlier when I first held the knife, I felt invincible."

"And so you think you projected those images?"

"I doubt it. I think it's more you than me. My mom had a different vision of invincible than you did." I smiled and shrugged. "For a moment there, I thought you'd project a supermodel."

Her cheeks bloomed, and she grinned. "If you had come in a minute earlier, you would have gotten an eyeful."

"Yeah, well, the pink lace is a nice touch." I couldn't help but smirk.

CHAPTER 23

MY MOTHER SAT, pale and silent, as I relayed the account of today's events and I knew she wasn't pleased. The thin lips pressed together, the hard stare, the pale skin marred by pink blotches were all signs of her discontent. But this time I didn't know if the anger was directed at me or just at the world in general.

"I knew I should have insisted that you come to church with me."

"You really think being in church would have made a difference?"

"Yes, then you wouldn't have gone through that."

"Come on, Mom. If we had gone to church with you and that reaper showed up there, it would have been a disaster. Besides, if anyone else dies that isn't on the list, Fate's going to be looking for me and I really don't want to see her again."

"What do you mean, see her again?" The sharpness in her tone rang through the room, and I bit my lip. I hadn't told her about Fate's brief visit.

"Fate delivered an ultimatum last night. It didn't thrill her that all those people died, and she blames me." The words rushed out like the air out of a cut balloon.

Her eyes narrowed. "You sure you weren't dreaming?"

"Yes, I'm sure." I glanced at Julia and nodded, returning my gaze to my mother. If she knew Julia was in my room in the middle of the night, I'd be in a boatload more trouble than I was right now. She'd eventually forgive me for not telling her about the visit with the elusive deity, but my girlfriend in my bedroom—that would warrant being grounded until summer, and I wanted to avoid that like the plague.

"Fate can't hurt you," Mom said.

"Yes she can, Mom. She can wipe out entire civilizations, and if I can't stop the reapers, that's exactly what she's going to do."

"She wouldn't dare."

"Who's going to stop her?"

"Your fa..." she stopped and snapped her mouth closed, glancing away from me.

"He's not around to stop her. Besides, he works for her. It's her list he's reaping."

The mood in the room shifted from dismal to downright dark, and I sighed. "Everything is going to be fine, Mom. Once I fix the mess I got us into, I'll go get my father."

Her gaze snapped to mine, and I knew what she was thinking. I knew from the paleness of her cheeks that she had already lost enough. If she lost me, that would throw her into a downward spiral that she was afraid she'd never recover from, which was just as undesirable as letting the rogue reapers declare all-out war.

"Julia didn't have any messages," I said, changing the subject. "Should we call the police?"

Mom blinked and turned her attention to Julia. "That's not a bad idea. Did you want me to call for you?"

Julia nodded. "Thank you, Mrs. Ramsay."

My mother stood and left the room, leaving me alone with Julia again.

"Thanks for not saying anything about last night," I whispered.

"I didn't want to get in trouble," she whispered back, watching the kitchen entrance for any sign of my mother.

"I have to figure out what to do with the knife tomorrow—I have a feeling I'm going to need it in school and I doubt my mother's going to let me bring it. I know if the school finds out I'm carrying a weapon, I'll get suspended." I combed my hand through my hair. "But I can't leave it here."

"Why not?"

"What if they know I have it? Wouldn't this be the first place you'd look?"

Julia glanced out the window toward her house and raised an eyebrow.

"I don't know. What if we can't get back into your house?"

"Well, what other option do you have?"

I had a lot of options, like attaching it to my ankle and wearing army boots and jeans to cover it up, or taping it to my stomach and wearing a sweatshirt, but I didn't think either would fly if my mother found out. "I'll figure it out," I said, not wanting to drag Julia into this further just in case I got caught.

"You'll figure what out?" my mother asked as she came back into the room.

I stared at her, my mind going blank and my palms breaking out in sweat. No answer came, and I turned toward Julia, silently pleading for her to intervene with something plausible and unsuspecting.

"We were trying to figure out what's going to happen with school this week," she said.

"We have Nick's grandmother's funeral, so I was going to keep him home for the wake and funeral."

With all the crazy things happening, I hadn't had time to deal with my grandmother's death, and the mention of the funeral yanked the air out of my lungs like a sucker punch. And I sank into the chair.

"And we have to help plan Julia's parents' funeral, so she'll be here for most of the week as well."

"What did the police say?" Julia asked, pulling me out of my own somber misery, and I took her hand, giving it a little squeeze before my mother answered.

"They identified the license plate, but until we called, they didn't know if anyone in the family survived. Now that they have the information, they can add your parents to the list of the missing people identified. They'll want to take a DNA sample from you to validate against the DNA samples they have to confirm your parents were indeed killed." She paused and glanced in my direction. "As far as what will happen from here, they'll send over a representative from social services, and

I'm not sure where it will go from there."

"Does that mean I'll have to leave York?" Julia said, and her hand clamped down on mine like a vise.

"I don't know. It depends on your family and what they want."

"Can I stay here?"

"We'll see what happens. I can't promise you anything right now, honey."

Julia's eyes filled with tears, and the pressure on my chest increased. The burn of my own tears blurred my vision, and I pulled her into my arms so she wouldn't see me lose it. Silently, I cursed God and everything in between Heaven and Hell.

CHAPTER 24

MY ALARM WENT off at six in the morning and I slammed my palm on the snooze button, unwilling to acknowledge another day. I wanted to go back a week, to before the floor fell out from beneath me. I wanted the carefree days of walking with Julia to catch the school bus and stealing a kiss in the hall. I wanted to know nothing of Fate and reapers and Death.

The knife vibrated under my pillow, prompting my eyes to fly open like shutters in a raging storm, and I wrapped my hand around the hilt, rolling off the mattress and facing the shadows.

I slid into the hallway and looked at the two doors, sensing which door the danger lay beyond. Again, my attention snapped to Julia's room, and I swung the door open, narrowing my eyes to adjust to the dark. She slept, unaware of the figure crossing the distance between the window and the bed.

"Don't even think about it," I said, and the cloak stopped, turning in my direction. "She's not on the list."

The reaper tossed a piece of paper in my direction and I caught the ancient papyrus in my hand, glancing at the directive scribed in the thin material. My heart thundered, and I slowly raised my gaze from the paper, crumpling it into dust. "I order you to leave her alone," I said, my voice a powerful growl, "or I'll end you." I lifted the glowing knife, pointing the tip in his direction. I didn't care what the paper said. Julia was not on the list, and there was no way I was letting this or any other reaper take her away on bogus orders. "I'll end anyone that comes after her, you understand?"

I swear the thing scowled, but it backed off, disappearing in a swirl of shadows.

I stared at Julia and my legs went numb. I sat hard, and the knife clattered to the floor in front of me, leaving a blackened mark where the hot steel scarred the floor. According to that paper, Julia was supposed to be in the car with her parents when the explosion went off on the highway.

I knew better. The rogue reapers caused that highway accident, and now they were handing out bogus directives? I needed someone on my side and I turned, heading back to my room.

I stood in the middle of the room, closing my eyes and concentrating. "Fate?" I whispered, conjuring up the image in my head.

"What do you want?"

I spun, facing her. "Was Julia supposed to be in that car?"

A crease appeared between Fate's eyes and she shook her head. "No, why?"

"They're handing out fake orders. Orders that have your seal."

I've seen my mother lose it before and I used to joke about her having a conniption—but it was nothing like Fate standing before me, transforming from beauty into rage.

Her rage turned the sky outside my window black with angry clouds and continuous bolts of lightning and rumbling thunder. The wind picked up, and I glanced from the window to Fate.

"Who dares to forge my name?" she spit the words out and her eyes took on the eerie quality of fire, while the room turned to ice.

"I think it was the reapers who took my father." My hand fell on the knife handle and the fear brewing in my belly, turning my stomach into a sourball, calmed. "I need your help."

"I told you, boy, this is on you."

"But they're using your seal to justify the killings." I tried to reason, but I could tell from the narrowing of her gaze that wasn't the right path.

She stepped closer, crowding me and I gripped the knife tight, staring her down and holding my ground. The blade throbbed against my thigh and I reached out with my empty hand, grabbing her by the wrist and dragging her into Julia's room where another reaper stood, ready to collect Julia's soul.

"Stop!" Fate ordered, and the reaper paused, his bony hand hovering inches from my future. "This is not written!"

The reaper's hand curled as he pulled it away. Cocking his head, he pulled out the written order from under his cloak. After taking a glance at the scribbles on the paper, he handed it to Fate and waited for further instruction.

Fate plucked it from his hand and scanned the words. She straightened her back and glared at the reaper. "Who gave this to you?"

"Promethis," he answered with a voice that reminded me of Darth Vader's without the heavy breathing.

"I should have known," she muttered and crumbled the paper, turning it to dust much like I did earlier. Casting her glare at the reaper, she stood stock straight. "Are you prepared to follow Promethis into the bowels of Hell?"

He shook his head and stepped away from the bed. "Promethis played me and I'm about as happy about this as you are."

"So will you help this boy defeat Promethis and his followers?" She waved toward me.

The creature nodded and turned his dead gaze in my direction and it fell on the knife in the sheath at my side. With a stumbling step, he backed away. "He has the sacred blade."

"Yes," Fate said without missing a beat. "He's Dylan's son. He has a right to the weapon."

If a skeleton could blink, I think this one did. His jaw dropped open, and then the air around him glimmered, sparking against the black sky beyond the window. The transformation from the cloaked skeleton to a teenage boy took seconds and ended with a pop like a lip smack.

The reaper reached into his coat and pulled out another sheet, handing it to Fate with trepidation. "I'm not sure we can stop this."

I glanced at Julia and her wide-eyed gaze met mine and then bounced between Fate and the reaper, and I wondered if she saw the metamorphosis from reaper to boy or not. When Fate glanced in her direction, she shut her eyes, pretending to be asleep, but she didn't fool anyone.

However, Fate was busy reading and when she looked up, those red blotches in her cheeks burned hot. Without a word, she handed me the paper and when I glanced at the next directive; I reached for the side of the bed, sitting heavily before my legs gave out.

"Memorial Day?"

"If you don't stop this from happening, I'll wipe the entire east coast off the map." She spun and, with a clap of thunder, disappeared.

CHAPTER 25

I SAT IN the living room, re-reading the sheet of paper, and I looked at the kid next to me. "What's your name?" I asked, now that the shock was wearing off.

"Lazarus," he said, his voice still deep and nothing like a teenager's should sound like.

The irony of the name struck a chord, and I stared at him, wondering if he was the Lazarus the Bible talks about.

He laughed at me. "Sorry to disappoint you, son, but I'm a lot older than the Lazarus you're thinking about." He glanced toward the stairs and I followed his gaze.

Julia stood on the landing, just watching us, her gaze bouncing between the odd man-boy and me. "Your mom's awake."

"This is Lazarus," I said, waving at the kid next to me.

"I heard." Julia stepped off the landing and crossed to me, wrapping her arm around mine. "Thank you," she whispered in my ear and kissed my cheek.

"For?"

"For saving my life twice this morning."

I nodded and glanced at Lazarus. "Looks like the rogues have taken things to another level,"

Lazarus chuckled and shook his head, crossing to the window. "They've got the ranks completely snowed, too. They told us Death deserted his post and gave us Fate's list. Except it really isn't her list. It's a fake aimed at pissing her off."

"What's happening on Memorial Day?"

"According to the directive, there's going to be an explosion at the fireworks display that will take out most of this town," Lazarus said. "Over a hundred reapers are on standby for this, and they all think it's part of Fate's playbook."

"And no one questioned it?"

Lazarus stared at me. "Disasters occur all the time, or don't you pay attention to what's going on in the world around you?"

My initial response wasn't appropriate, and I clamped my mouth closed, stifling the harsh words. Instead, I asked, "So how do we stop it?"

"The only thing I can think of is for you to address the reapers."

I raised an eyebrow, and my mind flooded with the nightmare and the leagues of angry reapers. His suggestion didn't sit well. It didn't feel right and all I could think was, *this is a trap.* "I don't think so," I answered.

The muscles in Lazarus' face jumped, tightening to hard knots that equaled his glare. "You think..."

I held up my hand, stopping the beginning of his rant. "Look, I don't know whose side you're really on. All I know is you came in here to take my girlfriend away, and when Fate intervened, you complied to save your ass. That doesn't mean I trust you." My fingers sought the blade hanging on my thigh and the reassurance of its powers.

"Dylan Nicholas Ramsay."

The admonishment came from the stairwell, and I turned, taking in my mother's unhappy stare. "What?"

"Language?"

Oh, for Christ's sake! I rolled my eyes and nodded. "Sorry, Mom. This is Lazarus. He's a reaper."

Her face blanched, and she shot her gaze in his direction. "What are you doing here?" And then on the heels of that question, "Why can I see you?"

Lazarus bowed in her direction, like she was the royal queen. "Ma'am, it's a pleasure to meet you."

My mother stopped at the base of the stairs, her eyebrows expressing an arch of surprise before they settled into their normal inquiring line. "You didn't answer my question," she said, ignoring the salutation.

"I, uh," Lazarus stuttered, glancing from my mother to me and back. "Fate asked me to look after your son," he said, waving a hand in my direction like an awful actor missing a cue on stage.

"From what I know, Fate and Death haven't been on speaking terms for quite some time now. Why would she suddenly have any interest in the wellbeing of Death's son?"

Lazarus blinked, his gaze bouncing as he tried to formulate an answer that would appease my mother. "Perhaps it is because your son is at the heart of a reaper civil war?"

"Bull," my mom said. "She's just as likely to take over the ranks and destroy humanity as some of the reapers."

"What makes you think that?"

"She's been gunning for my son ever since he was born."

"That's not true," Lazarus snapped. "She's just leery of him because he's the only child in the history of the royal bloodline whose Fate is not yet written."

Surprise knocked me back a step. "I thought everything until the end of time was already written."

"Yes, it is, with one exception. You. That's what happens when you've been resurrected from the dead—which puts a little kink in the overall plan."

"What are you talking about? Nick never died," my mother sputtered.

"You aren't exactly on the map either," Lazarus said to my mother.

"Why didn't Isabel tell me this?" I asked.

"I don't know." Lazarus turned back to my mother. "Fate's plan dictated that you and your son die on September 11, 2001. But Dylan made a deal, and took his rightful place as Death in exchange for your lives, so there is some bad blood between Death and Fate, especially where Nick is concerned."

"I was home with Nick," my mother started and glanced at me.

I looked away, at anything but her imploring eyes.

"Nicky?"

I hated when she called me that, and I glanced at her, nodding. "Isabel told me we died," I said. "But she didn't tell me it was already written in Fate's book that way." I turned back to Lazarus. "So, is this something that needs correcting, like my grandmother? Is that why everyone is up in arms about me ordering the reapers away from her?"

Lazarus shook his head. "No." He shifted his weight and glanced out the window. "But the rumblings of you being able to order us around from this side of the grave have made quite a few reapers nervous."

"Did you know who I was when you saw me upstairs?" I ignored the open-mouthed look my mother gave me.

"No."

"Didn't you wonder why I had Fate with me?"

"To tell you the truth, I was shocked beyond reason. No living human has ever had the audacity to call on her, never mind drag her around by the wrist like a child at show-and-tell."

"You called Fate?" my mother gasped.

"Yes, because the first reaper to come after Julia had a bogus order. I thought she should know."

"She was in this house?"

"Yes, Mom. She stopped Lazarus from taking Julia, and that's how we found out about the Memorial Day massacre," I said. "She said I had to stop it, otherwise she'd wipe out the entire eastern seaboard."

"No pressure or anything," Julia added.

"What exactly is the Memorial Day massacre?" my mother asked.

"The reapers are planning on wiping out the entire town of York on Memorial Day."

My mom sat down on the couch and ran her hand through her hair-a familiar action that I mimic when I'm perplexed. She looked up at me and then moved her gaze to Julia and Lazarus last. When she spoke, I almost laughed. She said, "I think I need a drink."

CHAPTER 26

JUST FOR THE record, funerals suck.

My grandmother's wasn't that bad, but then again, she was old and it was sort of expected. But the funeral for Julia's parents was a nightmare. Everyone cried, saying they died so young, so tragically. Little did they know her parents weren't supposed to die yet, so tragic was an extremely appropriate word to describe the situation.

The weight of the blame lay on my shoulders. If I hadn't ordered the reaper away from my grandmother, the sequence of events leading up to the disaster wouldn't have happened and her parents would still be alive.

Guilt bit at me, silencing any support I could give Julia. Instead, I sat in the pew holding her hand and stared at the floor, blocking out the priest and the eulogies. Tears burned my eyes and throat and at the end of the service, Julia yanked me from my reverie with four simple words, "It's not your fault."

Her whisper drew across my skin like a knife, and I met her gaze. "Yes, it is. Everything that's happened since my grandmother landed in the hospital is my fault." My father, her parents, Isabel, and now possibly millions of people.

I had no idea how to stop the reapers, and Lazarus's only offering was to gather the reapers together so I could address them. Maybe he was right. Maybe if I spoke to them, I could avoid the upcoming disaster.

The thing that kept me from agreeing to this was that stupid nightmare. An angry mob of reapers wanted me dead, and that wasn't something I could defend against, even with the knife on my hip or my limited martial arts training.

When the service was over, Julia made me stand with her in the procession line as the litany of distant relatives, acquaintances, teachers and school friends passed by offering condolences that would never erase the pain. She held up better than I did, perhaps because for her it was all still too surreal.

After the funeral, folks gathered at her house, and she and I slipped out back away from the din. I took a seat on the swing set and she joined me, swinging lazily back and forth, the creak of the chains offering little in the way of communication.

"I'm ready to go back to school," I said.

"Really?"

"Yeah, I just want things to be normal again." My sentiment produced a quiet laugh, and I shrugged in response. But she was right. Nothing was ever going to be normal again, no matter how much I wanted it to be.

"Maybe school will be good for us," she said after a while.

"And maybe it'll be a disaster," I mumbled under my breath. The proverbial hourglass was emptying faster than I could account for and if I didn't come up with a logical strategy, it wouldn't matter anymore. I'd be just as dead as Julia and the rest of the town and the bloodline would finally be severed.

Lazarus approached from my yard, and he took a seat on the end of the slide. He had been scarce since the confrontation with my mom earlier in the week and I didn't know what he wanted with us now. He started to speak and then shut his mouth and studied the clouds in the sky. "I'm sorry for your loss," he finally said, and glanced at Julia.

"Thanks," she replied.

"Did you find out anything?" I asked.

He sighed. "I was able to convince a handful of reapers that the orders that Promethis gave them were bogus. They are still skittish about any sort of mutiny, and wanted to know where Death was." He met my gaze. "Do you know where he is?"

"He's in Purgatory, being guarded by Leviathan."

His eyes widened and his complexion crossed from rosy-cheeked to pallid. "Leviathan?"

"Yup. That's what killed Isabel."

"Are you sure he's still...intact?"

I loved the way he put that. Intact. As if the man wasn't alive. "I'm here, aren't I?"

"That doesn't mean a thing."

"Isabel said as long as he's alive, I'm in danger. If my father was dead, the job would default to me. I'd be Death if he was already dead. Is that wrong?"

Lazarus stared at the ground. "No, that's not wrong," he said.

He left it at that, even though I sensed more. I didn't push it because right now I was tapped out and any more bad news would darken my already gloomy mood. But the sun was shining, and I needed some fresh air away from all this. "Want to skip out and go to the beach?" I said to Julia.

She glanced at her house and the debate was brief; she turned back to me with a nod and stood, ditching her dress shoes and leading the way through the path in her backyard. It wound between the houses, coming out near the high school and Long Sands road beyond.

The tide was out, leaving a considerable stretch of sand and we trotted down the stairs, heading across the gray pebbles to the hard packed sand and the swell of waves beyond. I left my shoes and socks at the edge of the rocks and relished the cool caress of the sand. I knew the water at this time of year was numbing, but I didn't care. It reminded me I was indeed alive.

Julia had more tolerance for the cold than I did and she stepped in to her calves, crossing her arms and shivering from the chill. I stayed in the shallow water, knowing if I ruined another pair of dress pants in the salty water, my mother would pitch a fit.

After a few minutes of watching her shoulders shake, I bent and rolled up my trousers, wading in next to her and ignoring the numbing sting. As I stepped beside her, she turned her tear-stained face in my direction and a little piece of me died.

The pain in her eyes shot through me and all I could do was pull her into a warm hug, holding her through the onslaught of sobs. I couldn't even tell her it would be okay because even if we made it through this weekend, the end of the school year loomed and beyond that was the great unknown.

CHAPTER 27

JULIA AND I stepped onto the bus Friday morning, subdued and quiet, but also relieved to be out of the morbid mood of both our houses. Even though it was a half day before the holiday weekend, it was still a half day with our friends. I just hoped the principal wouldn't pull us all into a lame assembly to talk about the tragic accident. If he did that, I might just lose it and that wouldn't be a pretty situation.

To my relief, the only mention of the numerous funerals was a highly unusual request for a prayer during the daily moment of silence, along with the standard offer of an open door with the school psychologist for anyone who needed it.

The alarms started an hour before dismissal and I stiffened in my seat, my gaze snapping to the window. Fear jumpstarted my heart at the sight of so many reapers and beyond the sea of black, the sky swirled. I sprinted out of my seat, through the classroom door, skidding in the hallway as I bolted toward the exit. I needed to stop whatever they were conjuring.

Vibrations and heat radiated from the knife taped to my back and a teacher reached to stop my progression. I spun out of the way, ducking under his grasp and slamming into the doors, tumbling onto the steps. I stopped in my tracks with the hilt of the blade in my hand, but still hidden by my shirt.

"Stop!" I yelled and the sea of black turned in my direction. Their glowing eyes pierced mine, sending shivers up my spine. Lightning split the sky and in the time it took to blink, I had the knife out, blocking the path of the bolt. The charge sank into the blade, vibrating up my arm and I pointed it toward the funnel cloud, sending the collected power into the twister. Wind and rain exploded outward in a blinding sheet, erasing the sea of reapers and leaving no remnants of the tornado behind. Only wispy clouds and the beginnings of a rainbow painted the sky.

Stunned, I lowered the blade before anyone inside could see, sheathing it and turning back toward the door in my dripping clothes. I expected an audience, but no one stood with their noses to the glass. I closed my eyes and blew out the breath I didn't know I was holding. Relief flooded through me and I trudged back to the building, trying each door, one after the other, and only finding resistance.

Lock down.

Which meant everyone was in the basement under the gym where they were supposed to be and right now, Principal Murdock was doing a head count. I took a seat on the steps and waited for the alarms to subside and the doors to release.

Lazarus appeared from around the corner of the school. I stared at him as he approached and took a seat next to me.

"What in the name of Heaven just happened?" I asked, still trying to come to grips with what I just did.

"I'm not sure."

"Oh, well, that makes me feel so much better."

"I'm serious. I've never, in all the millennia I've existed, ever seen anything like that. You erased the tornado they cooked up."

"And the reapers."

He shook his head. "No. You just scared the daylights out of them and they scattered. I'm sure they ran to Promethis to report what happened here."

"Oh." I picked at a hangnail and sighed. "Lightning hit the knife."

"That's not unusual."

I glanced at him and raised an eyebrow. "Say what?"

"The knife absorbs energy. It's a natural lightning rod."

"Thanks for telling me that." I rolled my eyes. That's all I needed, to be a walking, talking, lightning rod. "What would have happened if it hit me instead of the knife?"

Lazarus glanced away. "You do not want to know."

I let that settle, and a shiver traversed my spine. "So, was I the target?"

He studied his hands and slid his gaze back to me. "I honestly don't know. I'm not welcome in the ranks and the few that are still talking to me aren't discussing Promethis' plans."

I looked at the sky and then back to Lazarus, an idea forming, dawning, spawning, and I smiled. "Think I can do something like this again?" I twirled my index finger at the sky.

I saw a fraction of hesitation in Lazarus and then a hint of a shrug. "I don't know. I'm all out of ideas, kid. Your only choice might be to kill Promethis, but now that he knows you have the knife, I wouldn't be surprised if he avoided you like the plague."

CHAPTER 28

LAZARUS DISAPPEARED WHEN the alarms ceased. I sat still on the steps, dripping and pondering my choices, none of which settled well in my already knotted stomach. I didn't turn around when the doors burst open and Principal Murdock's angry voice bellowed over me.

"Dylan Nicholas Ramsay! When the alarms go off, that doesn't mean you can run pell-mell all over the property."

I was already angry with the situation, so I wasn't exactly in the mood for the principal or his condescending tone. I turned and glared at him, biting down on my tongue so none of the more derogatory comments slipped out - especially the one that would make him gasp and land me in deeper trouble than I'd ever been in before.

His eyes narrowed. "You're soaking wet."

"No duh." I climbed to my feet.

"Don't get smart with me or..."

The anger bubbled to the surface, unlatching the lock I had on my tongue. "Or what? You'll call my mother? You'll put me in detention?" Like his empty threats made any difference with what I was facing.

"Nick?"

My head snapped toward the soft voice and my gaze locked with Julia's. In an instant, the volatile lava in my soul calmed into a cool river, and I sighed, closing my eyes for a moment before I looked at Principal Murdock. "I'm sorry. The weather freaked me out a little..."

His red face lightened, and he nodded. "You still can't run out when the lockdown alarm goes off."

I nodded and dropped my gaze, making my way back in the school. I cast a sideways glance at Julia as I passed, and without being told, I made my way to the office for whatever punishment was in order.

CHAPTER 29

"WHAT WERE YOU thinking?" My mother paced the living room while I sat on the couch staring at her feet. "Look at me!"

Reluctantly, I raised my gaze, meeting hers. "I stopped them, Mom."

"But what if you couldn't? What if that tornado was planned? What if it was supposed to happen?"

I didn't have an answer for her, not one that I could share without getting grounded for life, so I shrugged.

"Nick, you have got to be careful. You are not immortal. You're not a god."

"I know, Mom," I said. "But I knew this wasn't pl..."

"How?" she interrupted.

I clamped my lips tight and inhaled. She thought I hid the knife in my room, and I knew the next words would cause more trouble, but I had to let her know. I had to get her permission to carry it over the weekend. "The knife."

Her eyes widened, and I bit the inside of my cheek, waiting for the conniption.

"The what?" Even the inflection of her voice made the hair stand up on my neck.

"The knife," I whispered and dropped my gaze. "It's taped to my chest, and I used it to stop the storm."

She folded into the chair opposite me almost in a rag-doll flop, her slack jaw telling me just as much as the slump of her shoulders. It was the first time in my life that I had blatantly lied to her. Half-truths and little white lies, yeah, like all the other kids I know, I've told them and I've been caught, but never a blatant lie. Before today, if she asked me a question outright, I told the truth, no matter the consequences.

However, this morning, when she asked if I had the knife with me, I lied. I told her I hid it somewhere in the house, but I wouldn't tell her where. She would not let me bring it to school, and I knew deep down that I needed it. I just didn't realize how important this hunk of metal really was.

"I explicitly forbade you from bringing that to school," she snapped when she regained her composure.

I fidgeted under her angry stare. "I know, but..."

"No buts—go to your room." She popped to her feet and pointed toward the stairs.

I learned a long time ago when she held that angry, unreasonable tone, to not argue. Arguing when she was like this was futile and would land me in deeper trouble than I already was.

"And you're grounded until further notice."

I stopped and spun on the landing, my jaw open in the same manner hers had been a few minutes ago. "You can't..."

"Yes, I can. Now go!" She continued to point toward the stairway and her face turned that deep shade of red, signaling I had pushed her too far.

I spun and vaulted up the stairs, slamming my door on any further comments. My heart drummed against my chest as my anger built, banging and making the rest of my skin tingle. My fists clenched and instead of taking deep breaths and counting to ten like I usually did to calm my temper, I let out a roar and swept the contents of my desk onto the floor.

I wanted to scream, to hit, to destroy.

The more I smashed, the bigger the fury grew. When my tables were clear of clutter and my floor was strewn with broken bits of glass and twisted metal, I finally sat on my skewed mattress, gasping for air. I scanned the room through a sheen of tears and collapsed back on my bed, feeling hollow and alone.

I don't know how long it was before my door opened, but the bedspread behind my head was damp with tears of futility and frustration. I didn't turn to see my mother's expected expression, her shock and anger at my senseless destruction. I knew the look, and I didn't want to see it right now. The door closed without comment and I closed my eyes, slinging my arm across them to block out the remaining daylight.

"Nick?"

I shot to a sitting position and stared at Julia and then glanced around the room with a huff. "I guess I lost it."

She smiled, raising her eyebrows and surveying the damage. "That's an understatement."

"Does my mom know you're here?"

She glanced out the window and shrugged. "She's down at my house unloading to my aunt."

"Ah. Does she know I destroyed the room?"

Julia shook her head. "You really think she'd leave the house while you were freaking out?"

She had a point. If my mother had been here, she would have been in my face the moment the first item broke. "No." I slowly sat back on the bed and wiped my face. "Can you grab the broom and dustpan in the hall closet?"

"Sure." She stepped out of the room, returning a couple minutes later and sweeping a clean path between the door and the bed before handing both the broom and dustpan to me.

"Thanks." I took the broom and cleaned up the broken glass, salvaging pictures from the ruined frames and chucking the rest. The garbage can wasn't big enough to hold all the broken bits, and I grabbed the can from the bathroom, filling that to the brim as well before replacing the few items I hadn't smashed on the shelves. I leaned the broom against the wall along with the dustpan and took a seat next to Julia on the bed. "How mad do you think she's going to be?" I asked.

"I'm not sure I want to be here when she comes back," Julia answered and bumped her shoulder into me.

I continued to stare at the broken knick-knacks, and I sighed, turning my gaze to her. "You know what?"

"What?"

"I don't really care." I took her face in my hands, planting a kiss. If I was going to die in two days, I was going to go in style, without fear of reprimand.

Julia had other ideas. She pushed me away, her cheeks flushed and her breath labored like I stole it away. "What are you doing?"

I grinned and raised an eyebrow. "You said my mom was at your house."

She smacked my shoulder, and I pulled her close, giving her a full kiss like they did in the movies, tongue and all. She melted into me, her arms tightening around my neck. Her heart pounded hard enough that I felt it on my chest and, as our tongues intertwined, the world disappeared.

"What the Hell are you two doing?"

The screech separated us like a catapult, and I was standing by the window before I could catch my breath. I met my mother's glare, gulping the sudden lump of fear, inhaling as it burned a path to my stomach.

Trouble didn't begin to describe this situation, and despite my earlier declaration, I found I cared a great deal and I could feel the excuses bubbling up with a tinge of bile; I swallowed it. Glancing at Julia, I took a deep breath, calming my pinging heart and preparing my ultimatum. "We're all going to die on Monday, so I figured, what the Hell."

After the words tumbled from my lips, I nearly gasped, but instead I shifted my weight and stood tall, holding my ground.

"Julia, it's time for you to go," my mother said without breaking eye contact with me.

I would not be the first to break eye contact, but from the sound of things, I knew Julia hightailed it out of the house faster than she had the day she first saw my father. Neither my mother nor I moved at first, but the bang of the front door seemed to break her paralysis and she crossed, trying to tower over me, which was a laugh because I had at least two inches on her. Even so, she could be intimidating, and she was bringing out the big guns tonight.

"You are in big trouble."

I laughed and the sting of flesh meeting my cheek shocked me into reason. My hand flew to the hot spot where my mother slapped me and I returned my gaze to hers, conceding by taking a step back. "If you don't let me go to the fireworks on Monday to stop the reapers, a lot of people are going to die." I started and before she could interrupt, I added, "If I didn't have the knife on me today, most of the kids at school would have died." I pulled the blade from the sheath. "This stopped the tornado."

Her gaze dropped to the shiny blade.

"It was huge, Mom. Big enough to annihilate the school and they sent it to kill me. Me and everyone else in that school." I lowered the knife, putting it back in the leather holder on my hip. "There were hundreds of reapers outside the school just waiting for us to die." I paused, and she shivered. I offered her a small smile as both a silent apology and to let her know I didn't have a choice, I had to intervene. I had to stop what they set in motion. "Don't you get it? They will not stop unless I can fix this, and if I can't, it won't matter much to any of us."

CHAPTER 30

"I DON'T THINK that's such a good idea," I said, focusing on Lazarus. "The last time I stood in front of a sea of reapers, they weren't too happy with me."

"I told them you wanted to talk."

I rolled my eyes. Lazarus didn't get it, or maybe he did, and I was just blind to his intentions. I knew he was walking me into the lion's den, but what I didn't know was whether he was on my side, or if they had contracted him to deliver me to my death?

"I've told you before, this just doesn't feel right."

"If you want to stop this…"

My glare shut him up. "Why are you so hot to have me address the ranks?"

The direct question caught Lazarus off guard, and his mouth popped open and closed like a guppy out of water. "I believe the best way to win this battle is through talking it out and not further splintering the sides," he said once he regained his composure.

"Look, I think your heart's in the right place," I started, giving him the benefit of the doubt, "but it's way too dangerous, especially if I'm on their ground." My fingers dropped to the hilt of the knife, feeling for the reassuring vibrations I had gotten used to when it felt I was doing the right thing. It lay silent, dormant on my thigh, like it was only just a plain kitchen knife instead of a supernatural tool designated to help lead the way. "I think I have some control here, but in your realm? Not so much."

"I've got your back," Lazarus said.

Doubt clouded my mind, and I sighed, unsure of what to do next.

"I know you're having a tough time trusting me, but I'm on your side. I don't want to see the Death and destruction that Promethis is planning. It's diabolical."

I bit my lip and looked out the window. Unease settled in the air, and I shifted my weight before speaking. "What do you want me to say?" I returned my attention to the reaper.

Lazarus offered a shrug.

"Well, that's helpful." I turned away from him and crossed to the kitchen in search of some food. If I was walking into the depths of Hell today, I didn't want it to be on an empty stomach. As I stacked roast beef on bread, I glanced at Lazarus. "You want something to eat?"

His gaze dropped to the array of food on the counter and then back to me with a raised eyebrow. "You know this is just a glamor, right?" He waved to his form like a magician in a magic show.

I stopped in the middle of squeezing the mustard and stared at him with a laugh on my lips. "I just figured since you took the form of a human, you might also have an appetite, too." I shrugged and finished making my sandwich. With a drink and an overflowing plate, I took a seat at the table and dug in, ignoring the imploring stare of my constant companion.

"Are you..."

I glared a warning, and he dropped whatever line of questioning he started.

When I finished and wiped my mouth with the napkin, I leaned back in the chair and gave a single nod. Lazarus hesitated, and I cocked my head. "You don't want to go now?"

"You're just going to leave that mess for your mother?" he asked with a wave toward the counter.

Sometimes I forgot Lazarus was ancient, but he had a point-one that my mother made to me whenever she was around. Clean up my mess. "Fine," I said, adding an eye-roll to the equation as I stood and started the tedious job of cleaning the kitchen. When everything sparkled, I turned. "Better?"

He smiled and nodded.

I wiped my hands and sighed. "So, how does this work?"

Lazarus stepped closer and clasped my wrist in his hand. Cold shot from my wrist up my arm like a creeping disease and Lazarus pulled. In a blink, the kitchen disappeared and the ledge I was on in my nightmare appeared before me, along with the hostile gaze of thousands of reapers. My throat tightened in response and the chill enveloped my entire form, leaving me numb and frightened to the core of my soul.

"Go ahead," Lazarus whispered from his perch next to me.

I glanced at the cloaked skeleton grasping my wrist and wished the glamor worked here because this being with a Death grip on me scared me just as much as the crowd gathered before me. I wished for Isabel and closed my eyes to gather the strength to find my voice. "Is Promethis here?" The question barely registered, but when I opened my eyes, I saw Lazarus shaking his head.

I could deal better with that than with the reaper gunning for me, riling up the crowd. I inhaled and surveyed the sea of black. "Hi." I raised my hand in the universal greeting.

No one moved.

"I'm Nick."

Still no reaction, and I glanced at Lazarus for help. He just nodded for me to continue.

"Dylan's son," I added, and that produced a chain reaction that spread through the ranks like an invisible wave. "My father has been kidnapped, and I believe one of your fellow reapers is behind it. He's also been handing out fake death orders, and I know for a fact Fate is not too happy with the whole situation." I shifted my weight, uncomfortable with the sudden silence that settled. The air became oppressive, constricting around my chest like a notched belt pulled too far. Instinctively, I stepped back and the knife on my hip began vibrating its warning.

"I told you he would come with some lame subterfuge," Promethis bellowed from the far corner of the ledge. He stepped out of the shadows in his larger-than-life form and turned his hateful stare in my direction.

233

I withered under it, fear lacing my throat like some vile poison I couldn't swallow. I tried to speak, to refute his lies, but only a squeak of derision escaped my constricted chest. I took another step back and Lazarus' grip tightened, holding me in place. My head snapped in his direction and I saw the hazy image of his glamor. His gaze was trained on something behind me, and the crease between his eyebrows captured his angst.

I took a quick glance over my shoulder, and my heart dropped to my feet. Terror encompassed me at the unending gorge less than a step behind me. The nightmare bloomed, and I snapped my gaze back to the crowd and the clear malice radiating from them. This situation was a total loss and if we didn't get the Hell out of Dodge, I was sure I'd see where that never-ending pit went.

"Get me out of here, Lazarus," I whispered, and hated the way my voice shook.

His grip tightened painfully on my wrist as the crowd of reapers stormed the ledge.

CHAPTER 31

VERTIGO AND THE sensation of falling gripped me and I squeezed my eyes shut.

The soles of my shoes slapped the floor, sending a painful vibration up through my body, and I opened my eyes to my empty kitchen. My wrist throbbed, and the knife pulsed in the case and without thinking, I pulled it from the sheath and spun.

A hooded being stood behind me, reaching for me in that threatening manner I was becoming accustomed to, and without hesitation, I plunged the blade into the center of its ribcage. The pain filled wail echoed off the kitchen walls and I twisted the blade, finishing off the diabolical beast.

The reaper exploded into a whirlwind of dust, but that didn't override the shuffle behind me and I turned, already in fight mode with the knife brandished before me.

"Easy boy," Lazarus whispered, his hands in front of him in innocent defense.

My muscles clenched, taut and ready to strike, but my mind recognized the friendly face giving the stand down order. It took a moment to register, but when it did, relief flooded through my veins, chilling me and turning my body into a wobbly pool of flesh. I lowered the knife and took an uncertain step toward the table, but my legs wouldn't hold my weight. Lazarus caught me and helped me to a chair.

"Did I get him?" I asked, pointing the knife toward the dissipating dust.

"No. That wasn't Promethis." He dropped his gaze to the floor. "I'm sorry for putting you in danger. I honestly thought reasoning with them would work."

I wanted to say I told you so, but when I opened my mouth, "You didn't know," came out. I offered him a smile that said I was just fine, no harm, no foul. "How are we going to stop what they have planned tomorrow?"

He shook his head and slumped in the chair, looking every bit a teenager instead of an ancient being. I offered a quiet sigh. Before I could speak, the rattle of keys interrupted my train of thought. I turned toward the hallway and my mother walked into the kitchen and stopped in the doorway with a frown on her lips.

I glanced back toward where I killed the reaper and understood her unhappy expression. A thin layer of dirt covered the island and the counters.

"What happened in here?"

I met her questioning stare. "I killed another reaper."

Her gaze snapped to Lazarus. "You were supposed to watch after him," she said, pointing in my direction. "Where were you when this happened?"

"It's not his fault, Mom," I said in response to her accusatory tone, and when she turned her stark stare in my direction, I continued. "Besides, I'm the one with the knife, and I'm the one they're gunning for."

"He's the one assigned to protect you."

I laughed. "What do you expect Lazarus to do?"

"I expect him to protect you."

"Ma'am, I am doing my best," Lazarus said. "If I had gotten here a few seconds earlier, I would have taken care of it, but your son seems to have a sixth sense when something isn't right and a warrior's split-second reactions that give him an advantage."

"My son is only thirteen. He shouldn't have to have a warrior's reactions. He should be out playing baseball or soccer or surfing with his friends and not be the one responsible for stopping the apocalypse." She threw her pocketbook on the table and stormed from the room.

Lazarus and I exchanged a glance, and then I chased after her. I found her face down on her bed and when I placed my hand on her shoulder, tremors from her silent sobs resonated in my fingertips. "Mom, everything is going to be fine," I said, with a confidence I didn't feel.

She lifted her tear-stained face from the pillow and met my gaze. "You don't know that."

I shrugged and sat on the edge of the bed. "I promise I'll be okay." I almost laughed at the certainty in my tone and wondered if my mother would detect the lie.

I couldn't promise anything except that if I failed, it wouldn't matter.

Victory or Death.

That's about as strong a motivator as anything I've ever known and I stared into her deep brown eyes, offering a smile. "Trust me."

CHAPTER 32

THE THUMP OF the basketball on the asphalt seemed to clear my mind, and I took the jump shot, hitting nothing but net from the three-point line etched in the driveway. Lazarus caught the ball and passed it back to me. I wiped the sweat off my brow and set up for another shot, but Lazarus blocked and I spun out of the way, ducking under his arm and taking another shot.

"That's game." I retrieved the ball, bouncing it into the garage before lying down in a shady spot on the side lawn. Big fluffy clouds drifted in lazy clumps in the sky, creating discernable patterns before breaking up again.

Lazarus sat next to me, picking at the grass.

Neither of us spoke.

A shadow spread over us and I propped up on my elbows, meeting Julia's gaze as she approached. I hadn't seen her since she bolted from the house Friday night, and without a word, she stretched on the grass next to me and studied the clouds.

Silence prevailed, and I relaxed back on the ground, offering an arm for her to lie on, and she moved closer, using my shoulder as a pillow. I'm sure I didn't smell that great after an hour of one on one with Lazarus, but she didn't seem to mind.

I sighed, content to watch the emerging patterns for the time being. There was still half a day left before sundown and I was hell bent on enjoying it. I still had no clue how I was going to stop the explosion tonight.

Explosion.

Explosion equals energy.

I shot up to a sitting position like a rocket taking off.

"Energy." I glanced at Lazarus.

"What about it?"

I unclipped the knife and studied it before I met his gaze. "You said this absorbs energy." I twirled the blade in my fingers.

"Yes, but..." He fell silent and I could see my thought process catching up in the morphing of his expression. But then his excitement became shadowed and dark. "I see where you're going, son, but that is just as dangerous as standing in the middle of a lightning storm."

I raised my eyebrow, challenging him.

Julia sat up and crossed her legs. "What are you proposing?"

"I stopped the reapers at the school by using the energy from a lightning strike against them," I said. "I think I can do that again tonight."

"It's too dangerous," Lazarus argued. "It will absorb the energy, but then it compounds and if you can't hold on to it, the knife could unleash something ten times as powerful and then it won't just be York wiped from the map."

"I was able to make those reapers disappear along with the tornado, and no one was hurt."

"Yes, but being struck by lightning and harnessing an explosion are two completely different things."

"Lightning struck you?" Julia interrupted, and I nodded.

"I blocked it with the knife." I focused back on Lazarus. "Do you have a better idea?"

"No, I don't have a better idea, but I'm not sure you realize what directing that kind of energy will do."

His cautious tone pricked my interest and I willed him to explain.

"You realize, when you direct that power toward the reapers, this time you won't just be displacing them, like you did with the storm," Lazarus said.

"So?"

"You will destroy any reaper in the area."

I couldn't care less about the reapers sent to destroy my town, and I shrugged in response.

"Any reaper in the area," he said again, enunciating each word.

Julia got it before I did and her hand flew to her open mouth, covering the gasp. I turned toward her and her wide-eyed gaze triggered the answer. I shot my gaze toward Lazarus.

"Any reaper?"

He nodded, and I fell back on the ground, covering my face and cursing softly under my breath. "Is that why you don't want me to try this?"

"No."

I met his gaze. "Then why?"

"Because it could kill you, too."

I huffed and stared back at the clouds. "This sucks."

"Nick, please don't do it," Julia said.

I turned my head and stared at her tear-filled eyes. "I have to," I whispered and took her hand in mine, bringing it to my lips and planting a kiss on her knuckles. "And I need you to stay home tonight, or better yet, see if your aunt can take you down to Portsmouth to the mall or a movie or something."

She yanked her hand from mine, and the tears evaporated into an angry glare. "If you think for one second, I will not be standing by your side, you are out of your mind."

"Julia..."

"No Nick, I'm not staying home." She crossed her arms and stuck out her chin in that adorably defiant way I loved, but right now, it just fueled the fire.

"I..."

"Actually," Lazarus interrupted.

"Actually, what?" I wouldn't be railroaded by either of them.

"It might be safer for both Julia and your mother to be with you," he said.

"No. You're going to stay with them and keep them safe."

"I can't. If I so much as touch either of them, they'll die."

I had forgotten that little tidbit and slammed my fist into the ground in frustration. "So I not only have to sacrifice my friend, I now have to add worrying about my mother and girlfriend while I'm trying to save this town?"

"It appears so," Lazarus said.

A whole host of inappropriate responses bubbled up, but I clamped my lips shut and stood, heading toward the ocean and the quiet calm of the sea. Julia caught up with me after a few strides.

"I need some time alone," I said, and she stopped matching my stride. I didn't look back, instead I broke into a jog that turned into a sprint. Trying to outrun responsibility was a futile act and by the time I reached the shore, my chest burned with both exertion and the weight of what I had to do tonight.

I sat and untied my sneakers, ditching them near the high tide mark, and walked to the water line halfway down the beach. The frigid spring water bit at my toes, numbing them on contact, and I stepped further into the tide, relishing the burn of the cold against my bare ankles and calves. I stopped at my knees, letting the chill settle through me like a comforting blanket.

The line of boats had already begun to gather, heading one by one around The Nubble Lighthouse and out of sight. I was sure they already anchored the barge holding the fireworks at Short Sands beach and I wondered which one of the boats carried destruction as their copilot.

I nibbled on my lip, turning over the plan in my head. *I wish my dad was here.* The thought came from deep down in my psyche and I clenched my jaws, shaking it from my mind. I couldn't think about my father. Not now. Not with everything at stake.

If I survived this night, I'd figure out a way to get him away from Leviathan.

If.

A big, whopping if.

Doubt settled, blackening my mood as the sun dipped lower on the horizon. My last thought before I turned to head home drenched my skin with dread.

Can I really stop this?

CHAPTER 33

I WALKED ONTO THE green like a prisoner walking into the jail yard for the first time, lost and wary of the fact not one reaper was visible. My mother flanked me on the right, Julia on my left, and Lazarus followed behind. I scanned the growing crowd with my hand resting on the hilt of the knife, waiting for the worst.

Night settled faster than it did in the summer's height and we weaved our way to the boardwalk and the beach beyond. A ribbon barrier blocked off the beach from the gathering hoard and I glanced at the array of beach blankets and folding chairs littering the lawn in anticipation of the fireworks.

Low tide left a hefty stretch of beach before us and at least three football fields beyond the breaking waves sat the barge. I brought the binoculars to my eyes, scanning the two boats flanking the barge. They tied an empty dinghy to the right side of the barge and I wasn't able to see the contents below the rim of the boat, especially with the pale gray cover snapped over the aft section.

Another boat sat anchored on the other side, within reach of a small ladder. This one carried a small group of men tasked with lighting the display. I lowered the binoculars and turned toward Lazarus. "I'm not sure I'll be able to save everyone, especially the people on the other side of the barge." I handed him the binoculars.

He surveyed the sea and lowered the spyglasses, handing them back to me.

"Where are all the reapers?" I asked.

Lazarus turned and scanned the crowd, and his mouth formed a frown. "They're here, but they're all wearing glamours."

I turned toward the crowd, and my jaw dropped. I didn't know who was who, and my gaze shot to Lazarus. "How am I going to take them out if I don't know whether someone's a reaper or a person?"

Lazarus dropped his gaze to my hip. "Listen to the knife," he said.

My heart banged against my chest, and my palms broke out in sweat. Full panic mode took over, and it was ugly. I sat down on the edge of the boardwalk and leaned over, dropping my head to my knees to stop the rushing roar that filled my head. I squeezed my eyes closed, ignoring both Julia and my mother as they tried to gain my attention.

Breathe.

The word whispered in my ear, the tone familiar and calming. It took me a moment to recognize the voice, and I almost laughed. It was mine. My inner voice that always calms me before a game or a karate match and I listened, counting my breaths as I drew them in slowly and exhaled in the same manner.

The world stopped spinning, and I turned my face toward my mother. "I'm okay. I just needed a minute." I sat up, scanning the area again. "Let's go over there. It's in the shadows, and we have the rocks at our backs so no one can sneak up behind us."

"I don't think they'll let us go beyond the tape," my mother said, and I rolled my eyes and hopped to my feet. I walked the length of the walk, with them trailing behind me, and when I reached the corner where the rock wall cast a shadow, I jumped down on the sand and turned, putting my hand out to help Julia and my mother follow suit.

Lazarus was next.

I pointed for the three of them to slide by the cone and settle in the corner of an alcove and I stood watch, backing up only when they had disappeared into the shadow.

"Where do you think you're going?" The sharp words broke the quiet at this end of the beach and I turned, staring at a cop who stood with his arms crossed.

My hand dropped to the hilt of the knife, and I offered a smile. "I'm sorry, officer, but I think I dropped my iPod on the beach earlier today and I was just looking for it."

He took a step closer, and the knife started its warning vibration.

Something about using a cop as a glamor rubbed me wrong, and I straightened my back and gripped the handle of my knife. He reacted by dropping his hand to the butt of his gun. Motion behind him caught my attention, and I realized the officer wasn't the danger, but the dark figure behind him was.

"Duck," I snarled and actually felt the command escape in a rush of wind. The cop fell to his hands and knees and I launched the knife at the chest of the reaper. The blade pulsed with light and landed true, erasing the glamor and leaving a black cloak flailing in pain. The first note of the band drowned the wail of the reaper and I leaped over the crouching cop, grabbed the handle of the knife and twisted the blade into the reaper's bony ribs.

After the dust devil settled, I turned toward the kneeling police officer, sheathing the knife and shrugging. "I'm sorry."

His eyes kept jumping from the space behind me and back to me, and I could see the confusion muddled with terror in his eyes. "What was that?"

I bit my lip, glancing toward the crowd, and then looked at the ocean before bringing my gaze back to his. I had made the man duck. I felt the power leap from my chest and bend him to my will. It was a heady feeling and a responsibility I did not want.

"You never saw me or the reaper. Now move along," I whispered, hoping there was still a little of the unwanted capability left.

Like a good soldier, he blinked and turned away, wandering back toward the crowd.

I stared after him and then backed into the shadows, feeling for the cold rocks and praying no one on this side of the realm or on the other side saw that little display of power.

Unnerved, I sank to the sand and closed my eyes, counting each breath until the thumping in my chest abated. When I opened my eyes, Lazarus kneeled before me like a knight bowing to the king.

Utter annoyance braised through me, leaving a sour taste in my mouth. "Don't do that," I snapped and stood, walking farther into the shadows until I found my mother and Julia gawking at me with the same awe.

Now I just wanted to burrow in the sand and forget who I was. This little mind trip into the underworld was getting to me more than I thought and I glared toward the crowd, feeling the frustration burning in my chest like a fireball.

Night descended without another encounter and when the last note of the band played, I let the power thrumming in my stomach fill every pore until I tingled all over. I couldn't do this with Julia and my mother flanking me, so I gave them a nod. "Stay here."

My gaze traveled to Lazarus, and I made a decision based on loyalty. I issued an order, one he had no choice but to follow. "For the next hour, you are to stay at the top of Mount Kilimanjaro."

His expression registered shock, and then he disappeared with an audible pop.

I glanced back at my mom, and shock painted her face, but I shrugged. "I'm serious. Stay here no matter what." Before I left them at the rock wall, I stepped close to Julia and ran my hand across her cheek and into her hair, pulling her to me.

The kiss turned the burn in my soul into an inferno of determination, and I pulled away.

With a nod, I turned away from them, willing a cloak of invisibility around them so no human or reaper could see them besides me. I thought of the actual artifact from _Harry Potter_ and wished I had that cloak on hand to keep them safe. Instead, I had to rely on the shadows to keep them out of danger.

My eyesight adjusted to the dark, and I saw forms on the barge in the distance and the first spark of fire. I turned toward the crowd and unsheathed the pulsing knife. Pure power radiated through me. "Show yourselves, you cowards."

My cry to action worked, and the glamours wavered, splitting in the light of the first round of fireworks. I was on my home turf and not some random ledge in their realm, so when the first reaper charged, I was ready.

"Dust to dust," I whispered as the first fell. Three more followed and then the legion seemed to get the idea that individual attacks would cause their destruction, so they tried a coordinated attack.

I can't remember ever moving so fast in any of my belt tests and I'm sure I would have made my Sensei proud, but after the third wave, my arms felt like lead weights and the swirl of sand and Death surrounding me made catching my breath next to impossible.

The fireworks display continued and for a moment; I wondered if anyone in the crowd could see me doing some weird knife dance in the sand. I chuckled at the image I painted in my head and I scanned the legions of reapers that formed a big u-shape surrounding me.

"You can't stop this, boy." The sea of black parted and Promethis stepped forward.

"Want to make a bet?" The words sounded labored and tired, but resolute. I reset my form, just waiting for the next reaper to step into the ring with me.

"I'll see that bet and raise you." Promethis waved his bony hand to my right. The legion parted and the cop I coerced earlier stepped forward with my mother and Julia grasped in each hand. He forced them to their knees and pulled out his pistol, placing the barrel on Julia's temple, and waited for further instructions. "See, you aren't the only one that can control humans."

A sick sense of loss engulfed me and I stared into Julia's deep brown eyes. "Don't you dare," she whispered when I lowered the knife.

I inhaled the salty, firework-tinged air and looked up at the brightly painted sky before returning my glare to Promethis. I pointed the tip of the knife toward the officer. "It's not their time."

The statement hung in the air like the smoke from the fireworks.

"I've got the sheet that says otherwise," Promethis reached under his cloak.

I raised the knife to the sky, willing the heathens on the barge to trigger the explosion, praying the shock of setting it off earlier than they expected would buy me enough time to save my mother and Julia.

The sheer decibels of sound that followed nearly threw me onto the sand, and I stumbled, catching myself before I fell, the knife still aimed at the Heavens like a beacon. I glanced at the cop. "Drop the gun," I whispered, and the pistol tumbled to the sand at the same moment the energy from the explosion hit the blade.

Pain raced through my arm and I looked at the fiery knife in my grip, grinding my teeth and forcing myself to hold on, to control the power for long enough to harness and bend it to my will.

The line of reapers backed away even as the fireworks finale continued overhead, filling the sky with bright bangs. I lowered the vibrating blade, pointing the tip at Promethis.

"Dust to dust," I growled and aimed, concentrating on only the reaper hoard around me.

Like the energy that dispatched the tornado, this shot out like a hundred silver lightning bolts, striking the reapers down in one fell swoop and the sand devil that resulted flowed around the four of us in a funnel that nearly reached the lowest firework.

It exploded outward, raining a fine mist of sand over the crowd.

I stood, staring at all the people on their feet clapping and whooping and cheering, then the world spun into blackness.

CHAPTER 34

STEADY, RHYTHMIC BEATS brought me out of the dark recesses and I opened my eyes, blinking at the clear bag of liquid hanging above me. I tried to swallow, but my tongue stuck to the roof of my mouth. I coughed and blinked again, trying to lift my head, and I groaned, lifting my hand toward the pounding in my temple.

I stopped and stared at the bandage covering my hand and wrist, wondering what happened to leave me feeling like the school bus had run me over. I glanced toward the light and my gaze fell on my mother slumped in the chair by the window, sound asleep.

"Mom?" The word scraped my mouth painfully, and she opened her eyes at my distant croak.

"Nick," she said, straightening in the chair and scooting closer.

"Water."

She poured a glass from the pitcher on the nightstand and offered me the straw.

The cool liquid soothed my mouth and throat and I slumped back on the pillow, studying the ceiling, wondering if I dreamed everything. I couldn't formulate any of the questions pinging through my mind, they were all way too crazy, but when I dropped my gaze back to my mother's I saw the grain of truth in her eyes and in her mind and I clenched my jaw.

"It wasn't a dream?"

"No Nicky, it wasn't a dream."

I covered my eyes with my bandaged forearm and the ache in my chest grew, my chin quivered, and my throat burned with salty tears.

"Death is my father?"

"Yes."

"And I stopped the explosion?"

"Yes."

"No one died?"

Silence filled the room, and I lifted my arm, meeting her gaze. She looked at the floor and then back at me, and a crushing dread gripped my soul. Lazarus stepped out of the shadows and put his hand on my mother's shoulder.

"Mom." Tears blurred my eyes, and I blinked, my glance bouncing between them, and the hollow pit in the center of my body grew. "I'm sorry," I whispered.

She smiled, "Don't be sad, Nick, I'm here anytime you need me."

Panic hit, and the next question bolted out of my mouth. "What about Julia?"

"I saved her from the explosion," my mom said.

Relief flooded through me, and I glanced at Lazarus. "What about the knife?"

"It's in a safe place until you're ready," my mother whispered and patted her thigh.

The door squeaked open, pulling my attention away from my mother, and a figure slipped into the room. I recognized her immediately and offered a sniff and a smile. "Hi."

She froze for a moment and then crossed the room in a flurry of blond hair and hospital gown and she nearly threw herself across me in a giant hug. "Nick!"

Breathless from both pain and relief, I just wrapped my arms around her and buried my face in her hair, happy that she was alive and still happy to see me after all that went down.

I smoothed her hair and kissed her cheek, thankful for the feel of her warm skin and the hint of strawberries wafting from her hair. Small prayers were answered, and I bit my lip, blinking the sheen of tears away.

"Your mom," she whispered in my ear, her voice choked with emotion.

"I know." I glanced toward the empty chair, already missing her. "But I don't know why we're in the hospital."

"They said we were sitting in a restricted area and a few of the fireworks malfunctioned, acting like a loaded missile which struck the sand in front of where we were sitting. It exploded and killed your mother and knocked both of us out."

"And what do you remember?"

She stared at me for a long time and then sat up. "I remember you using the knife to absorb the explosion, and then there was a flash of light and your mother tackled me. When I came to, she was dead, and you were face down in the sand and the emergency crews were rushing onto the beach."

She took a deep breath. "I thought you were dead, too."

I reached out and wiped the tear from her cheek. "It's going to take a lot more than a few hundred reapers and a bomb to kill me."

My attempt at humor worked, and she cracked a smile.

"What happens now?"

"You think you might like to come to Florida with us?" she asked, raising an eyebrow that told me more than any words could.

I grinned in response. "But doesn't Florida have alligators?"

The End

* * * *

Continue The Death Chronicles with HIGHWAY TO HELL.

About the Authors

William F. Houle

Co-Author of The Death Chronicles Trilogy

At the time The Death Chronicles Trilogy was written, William F. Houle was a middle-school student with an amazing imagination.

When he approached his mother, author J.E. Taylor, with the idea for a trilogy about the son of Death, well, she couldn't resist the incredible story line William created and agreed to work with him to craft his idea into words.

Thus, *Don't Fear the Reaper* was born.

J.E. Taylor

J.E. Taylor is a USA Today bestselling author, a publisher, an editor, a manuscript formatter, a mother, a wife, a business analyst, and a Supernatural fangirl. Not necessarily in that order. She first sat down to seriously write in February of 2007 after her daughter asked:

"Mom, if you could do anything, what would you do?"

From that moment on, she hasn't looked back.

Besides being co-owner of Novel Concept Publishing, Ms. Taylor also moonlights as a Senior Editor of Allegory, an online venue for Science Fiction, Fantasy and Horror.

She lives in New Hampshire with her husband and during the summer months enjoys her weekends on the shore in southern Maine.

Visit her at www.jetaylor75.com and sign up for her newsletter for early previews of her upcoming books!

If you liked DON'T FEAR THE REAPER, check out the rest of THE DEATH CHRONICLES TRILOGY:

The Death Chronicles Trilogy:

The day Nick Ramsay's eighth-grade teacher drops dead in his classroom, Nick sees his first reaper. When another cloaked figure appears at his grandmother's bedside, Nick issues an order for the vile creature to leave her alone.

This simple act of defiance creates a domino effect that brings Fate and

Death to Nick's door. When his true lineage is revealed, his entire world is thrown into chaos.

To make matters worse, a group of rogue reapers declares war on humanity. If Nick cannot stop them, the resulting chain reaction will not only kill those closest to him, but the entire universe could end in a bloody battle.

The Death Chronicles Trilogy includes Don't Fear the Reaper, Highway to Hell, and Knocking on Heaven's Door.

THE DEATH
CHRONICLES II

Death is the family business, but not
one I want to pursue. Thankfully, it's
been passed down from father to son
for generations, so it should skip me as
Death's daughter. Then I won't have to
stop being alive and can actually live
my life. Right?

Well, the reapers don't agree. And
neither do the angels.

One thinks I'm destined to take over,
the other believes I will destroy
existence. Both want me dead to match
their own agendas.

I have an agenda of my own, and
Leviathan who has sworn to protect
me. But once my family and friends
start being targeted, the family
business, while grim, might be the only
choice I have to save those I love.

The Death Chronicles *II* includes the
following titles

Grim's Daughter

Finding Death

Reap the Dead

Kissing Fate

Find these titles and other fantasy
and suspense titles on J.E. Taylor's
website!

www.JETaylor75.com